BEST & BRIGHTEST 2012 ANTHOLOGY

by New Dawn Publishers Ltd

Edited by Sundeep Parhar

BEST & BRIGHTEST 2012 ANTHOLOGY

First published in 2012 by
New Dawn Publishers Ltd
292 Rochfords Gardens
Slough, Berkshire SL2 5XW

www.newdawnpublishersltd.co.uk

newdawnpublishersltd@gmail.com

ISBN 9781-908462-02-2

TABLE OF CONTENTS

Aedan Andrejus Burt was born in 1993, in Fife. He is currently a second-year undergraduate at the University of St Andrews, studying for a Joint Honours in Classical Studies and Philosophy. His interests are wide-ranging, from politics to psychology, societal and social trends to perceptions of the individual, both among and *contra* others.

Literature has always been a central focus of his life, particularly as it meaningfully reflects, explores, and suggests such concepts in a way which can immediately both be felt and understood. Whisky is Aedan Andrejus Burt's first work to enter publication, and he is proud to see it included in the *Best & Brightest 2012 Anthology*.

Whisky

In a southern sector of Edinburgh, there is a tall block of apartments, surrounded by traffic and with an old, rickety bridge behind. Grey, aged and dilapidated from the outside, they would seem to tell a different story from within, and each resident has at least tried to make his set of rooms his own - but it is an area of the utmost squalor and noise. On the fourth floor, a man has rented five rooms, has been living there for some years now; the only available accommodation.

At first, he thought he was lucky to find that one room - the central one, and no bigger than the others - was built as it was; the walls, all but one of them and a tiny section where a window sat, given over entirely to bookshelves - deep, and pressed into the wall like the libraries of the old aristocracy; but it was not long until he learned that this is no wise reason to take a set of rooms for any sort of minimum term - especially when one's finances were as low as his. Still, take the rooms he did, and he soon found himself spending most of his time in that room; and the conditions within and without, every day, just added to the past of his life that had served to age him so beyond his years.

It is hard to say that there was anything wrong with that room - some might even call it homely - but it is never healthy for a man to spend hours on end, from the early evening, every night, in a small and cramped room surrounded by books. At first, he would only spend the first few hours of the evening there, leaving for bed shortly after the early autumn sun would go down; but by the time winter came, when he would return in the half dark, or else in complete night, his first action on coming in would be to enter that room and draw those curtains before sitting on a chair to write; or else he would begin to read those precious volumes by which he found himself surrounded.

In truth, he could not understand why the previous owner had left them all there, or else why, if they had died, whomever had inherited considered himself to have no use for them, and hence simply left them to the place. Either way, it became like an addiction, and so in the winter, without the light of the sun of an evening to mark the passing of time, (a clock had never be installed in the room, and the new resident felt no willingness to bring that tyrant Time into the place), he began to pass whole nights there, either writing or reading, and wondered often how he would manage to get through to evening, tired as he was and with a need to go out on business for at least six hours in the day.

The light too, in that room, quickly became oppressive, the small window in the only wall without a floor-to-ceiling shelf hardly even giving enough light during the summer months, let alone in winter with its impenetrable darkness; and so the small electric light of the ceiling had to be used. It was an old light, regardless of the bulb that was put in, and its dirty, orange glare put him in mind of the streetlights outside, or the old gas lamps of the past; the stain of it making it an endless pressure on his mind. The size of that room too, was of not much help, it really being little more than an elongated box no more than ten feet long and seven wide. Indeed, although those shelves did not fill any of the room, a substantial writing table had been installed at its centre, seemingly an antique, that sold the rental of the apartments to him almost as much as those books.

Its legs were high, making it perfectly easy to get even a large seat underneath, although the man only ever used the antiquated wooden chair that he found there. Above was a short, rectangular section with two large drawers at the front, both of which he used, and above those, a large wooden section followed on which to lay the paper, sloping back at a comfortable angle; while a short, flat ledge was left at the top where ink could be positioned, or anything else a man might wish to have at his desk. A comfortable desk it certainly was, but its overall effect on the room was suffocating, claustrophobic, for with that their owner effectively sacrificed all other chairs, all conventional comfort, and condemned the room to a perpetual life of study. Indeed, there was nothing in front of the desk bar bookshelves, and nothing to either side, with it only easily being possible to move backwards from the desk, towards either the door or the back wall.

It was this that was the only wall not entirely covered in books, for a small section had been left free of shelving in its centre, some four feet wide, so that the wall itself was pushed back to form a little recess between the shelves. On his taking the apartment, the wall here was blank, white, and in stark contrast to the rest of the finely adorned room, for most of the volumes in their shelves dated back to Victoria's reign, still in their fine leather bindings; and that too, disturbed him, often subconsciously, every time he entered the room.

It was after several of these long nights, of many months trying to strive with the people in his new employment in this new city, that an even deeper disaffection with the world finally set in, and then he started to drink. It was not that he had not drunk already, of course, for what man of his age couldn't have; but simply that he began to use it as his sustenance, as a way of scorning his detestable world, this ridiculous society, that he had come to hate. At first, he would start his evenings in the first bar he could find, sit for a few hours, and then go home, for his books and work would call him; but he was a fast drinker, and in those few hours he could polish off many pints, glasses or measures.

When he began, it was always just beer, and then he found that that wouldn't take effect soon enough, would fill him with gas; and so he moved on to wine, drinking it like water in the same way he had the beer. Soon, though, that too seemed to take too long to be felt, and so he moved on to Pimms, straight; and after cycling through the liqueurs, everything that could ever have been described as moderately strong, he moved on to spirits. None did he like, but he always found they had the effect, until he finally found the heart to try the Scots' whisky. Effect, and taste - it was a paradise for him, for he had reached the stage months ago when he only felt right with a drink in him.

For nearly half a year, he went on thus: always coming home stumbling, and yet still feeling a need to spend his whole night in that study. Very rarely would he go to sleep; and rarer still in a bed. Soon, however, he became even more dissatisfied - dissatisfied with this routine, and still more so with the people he would see in those places; the drunks, the partygoers, the clubbers... Yet the drink was a part of him; but he still could not bear those surroundings, the people who frequented them, and what went on - and a part of him simply felt that he was betraying himself, even if he only spent two hours there, to be away from his books and work.

That was when he decided to do something about it - not to abandon his drinking, he couldn't - but to find a way to allow himself to drink, to free himself from this world he so much despised, and become calm; only in the place where he had his books, a table, and could write. A form of journalist now, a writer, and a contributor for four of the country's greatest universities; once he had been a soldier, wounded in the Gulf in the early stages of the conflict. Now it was only in his work that he could find any sense of fulfilment, and only in drink that he could even loosely associate with the world at large; and so he had wondered often, long before now, whether or not the paper he worked for knew, and if not how they couldn't, and also whether they would be firing him any day.

It was then, with these thoughts having played on his mind for the better part of a year now, that he decided that he needed to make himself able to drink at home, and then he started stockpiling the kitchen with bottles of the only whisky he would drink; but even the ten minute delay of having to get home before he could start added torment to his mind. At his desk too, this began to feel like the most ludicrous of solutions, for every time he wanted a drink, or else emptied a bottle, (if, that is, he had been sober enough to had have the forethought to bring the whole thing through with him), he still had the torturous task of stopping his work, getting up and dragging himself through to the kitchen, only to get a more whisky, too often in a glass, before coming back and finding his place once again. He would inevitably lose steam.

After carrying this through for a few weeks, the anguish and anxiety built up even more, and it was then that he finally remembered the gap between the two sections of shelf behind him, there, on the back wall, as he sat at his desk. The very next day, he was out searching the antique shops; that night, and then the next again, for five nights in a row - and somehow he stayed sober all this time, while his mind played upon the purchase of the one thing he felt was needed. In what must have been the fortieth shop and on the morning of the sixth day, a Saturday, when he had no work, he finally found it and installed it in that gap; the gap he had decided to fill with the highest degree of accuracy. His hope had been for a drinks cabinet, a large one with beautiful glass doors, from the same era as the desk and those bookshelves - and somehow he was not disappointed. There it had been, a drinks cabinet, of the perfect size to fit into that gap - the seller had even said that he had heard it had been taken from one of the apartments somewhere in the south of Edinburgh when its owner had died; and somehow it hadn't sold.

The price, almost as much as he had spent on whisky the previous week, and a quarter of his monthly wage, didn't seem to matter; and it was even better than he had hoped. The cabinet still came with all that it had contained: the large decanters, crystal, and of various shapes - spherical, cubic and even pyramidal; the goblets and tumblers, the nip glasses and flutes - all of the finest work, hand-crafted; and even silver stirring spoons which he wondered why he would ever need. In its entirety, it seemed perfect. It was this, then, that began to fill that gap on the back wall, and although he would still have to get up to refill his cup, whichever it may be, and the decanter he might use with it, the whole thing felt much more comfortable; for he had resented his seeming dependence on alcohol, his awareness of which had grown every step he took towards that kitchen or back.

And so his routine continued, hardly altered, for more than two years. He would return from the newspaper's office quickly, as soon as he could, yet all this while the delay this caused before he could get his first drink of the night played on his mind. Sometimes, he would even take a substantial hip flask into work, only to make the day pass a little quicker, for he even felt, had since the beginning, that his thoughts were more lucid in the first stages of drink. Then, he would go in quickly, often not even pausing to lock the doors, or even get himself some food, and go straight into his study, sometimes staggering already, just to get at some of the whisky in those decanters, even before he could sit down. After that, he just wrote, or else he read.

*

For more than four years now, the man has been living like this: going between work and the bottle, books and the pen; all with hardly a moment's rest. Tonight, the room looks like it is waiting for him. The curtain is already drawn against the night, left from the day before, and the light remains on, bearing down on the room with its dirty, orange glow. The door to that study is half closed, just slightly more than ajar, almost as if it has started to swing back after he closed it this morning with his trembling hand, the muscles flexing then more with tiredness than with the haze of drink; but even closing that door cannot bring any comfort to the room as it traps in the overbearing, almost tainted light.

All through the day, as always, the noises from below and the sides have continued to beat through the walls - the sounds of voices, footsteps and *life* - sometimes interspersed by the harsh sounds of cries and screams, as is common to any rundown area of a city. If he had known how thin the walls were too, it is unlikely he would have taken such a set of rooms - and yet this is what comes of taking a decision based solely on the sight of a single thing that one loves, without waiting first for all the information about what will await a person in the new circumstances they will choose.

At around eight o'clock, his footsteps are finally audible in that room, empty apart from the books, his desk and that cabinet; and the room has no sympathy, anywhere in its atmosphere, for the man who is slowly dragging himself, half stumbling, up his last stairs, the fourth of the building's six flights. For the first time in nearly two years, he has been at a pub, and the dank heaviness of drink clouds his mind and vision even before he reaches his rooms. On his way up the stairs, he is accosted by another man. Slouched and dirty, he sits on the edge of one of those stairs as if he intends to sleep there; and he has the wild and misty-eyed look of a drug addict about him as he raises his arms to the man going by on the stairs, begging him for 'money, anything, a fiver?', almost piteously; but the action makes his sleeve slip down to reveal the marks of the needles; and they raise a deep revulsion in the man, drunk as he is, as he waves the other off with some words he cannot even make out while continuing his ascent. Leaving the final step and moving onto the landing, the man realises he has not returned this drunk for a very long time.

With quick strides, he moves to his door, and the green painted wooden panel is still as he left it that morning. Slightly ajar, it swings back on its hinges with a harsh creak at his light touch; for he still has not found time to have the lock, broken since his second year here, replaced. Some days, it surprises him that his rooms have never been burgled, but he can only conclude that such a high flat in a poverty-ridden area would not tempt even the most desperate of thieves to look within. Once, he thought someone had been in, and yet nothing seemed to have been gone, and this he put down simply to the fact that his only possessions worth taking were the books, and that these are things in which few people see a value nowadays.

This night, as always, he goes straight into his study without even glancing around; and as soon as he gets in he goes straight to the wooden chair before that desk, practically falling into it, as a piece he wants to write, *has* to, comes back into his mind. He has been asked to contribute something to *The G---*, not his usual paper, for their social commentary and correspondence pages, and now he is in the perfect mood to begin on it, though he doubts it will be as optimistic as they seem to hope. Looking at the surface of the desk, he sees he still has the paper in place from the night before (he could never adjust to the idea of just typing a piece up, but liked instead to form a manuscript version first, and in ink, with one of those old pens that forever needs to be dipped into the pot to be able to write).

It is good quality stuff, and he is proud of it, as only a man can be of superfluous things; and his hand moves to the drawer on the right quickly in its accustomed, confident manner, almost to spite the drink. He pulls it open in a single, fluid motion; and there lies the pen, black, with its gold nib, and the finely styled pot of ink next to it, both of which he quickly takes out and places on the ledge above the sloped part of the desk. He takes the lid off the inkwell and glances at the paper there as he moves his pen towards the thick, dark substance; but then, just before the pen can touch it, he quickly lays it down next to the pot and slowly gets off that seat; for a dryness, real or otherwise, has become acutely perceptible on his tongue.

Despite the drunkenness, he turns quickly, automatically, to take the quick handful of steps that will bring him before the large bulk of the drinks cabinet at the back of the room. His hands move without thought, their movements spontaneous, as he undoes the latch and swings its doors open; and his mind is beyond the point of letting his eyes register the ornate carpentry of its wood, the weaving inlay, or the thick crystal corners of the square decanter for which he reaches; the fine workmanship which he had thought aristocratic, charming and beautiful when he first set eyes on it. No, now he has eyes only for the light brownish liquor inside; through which, as he carries it back to the desk with the large nip-glass beside, a single shaft of that dirty light shines, giving it the flickering colour of amber or a rich orange gold.

Reaching the desk, he places them down there firmly, on the flat plateau of its top, before lowering himself back down onto the seat. For a second, he looks at the paper, staring almost blankly before his hand gravitates once more, subconsciously, towards the pen. Picking it up, he moves it towards the inkwell again, following it with his eyes; but before the pen can receive its hundredth baptism, the whisky has again caught his eye, and the pen finds itself once more upon the wood of that ledge, discarded, as the stopper is quickly removed from its crystal setting. He reaches forward, now more than a little off his chair, and with the glass - really more of a wide, deep tumbler than any form of conventional nip-glass - in one hand and the decanter in the other, he begins to pour the rich, fiery liquid into the cup; and a part of his mind revels in the sound of the precious liquid flowing into the glass, filling it until the level is hardly more than two centimetres from the top.

His left hand he keeps on the decanter, clutching it possessively; while the right finds itself quickly wrapped around the glass, raising it to his lips where he takes a large gulp, polishing off some half of the liquid in one go, before he again fills his cup from the decanter. The feeling is good, relief instant; but habit still makes him give a quick shake of his head against the intoxication, useless as he knows it is, as the intensity of the drink courses down his throat; and then the thought of the paper, still unfilled, comes back into his mind, and he takes another sip, thinking, and another, before topping up his glass once more. Finally, then, he takes up the pen and dips it, straightening the paper again purely from habit, and begins to write through his bitter and inebriated haze:

'Now, where can I begin with what this world is now? With society? With our Britain? Can I use analogy, allegory? My God, there's no words that can describe what society is these days,

what we've let it become; and the people preach "progress". I look out on this city and I see nothing but decadence, degeneracy. How could anyone be happy living in a world like this?

'I know people, hundreds of people, but I *see*. I see them, eternally rushing about, always "busy", scuttling and running around as a great faceless mass, but do they ever stop to ask why? They go, cover the streets day and night, forever running, hurrying, and that is only ever to get some pointless place, sit a few minutes, maybe hours, and move on; never any purpose. Even in the morning, at rush hour, even those walking or driving to work – it's all for the same worthless cause. Day in, day out, they go in and work, but that's only for a few pounds to squander on the first thing that catches their eye as they walk out of the office once they've been paid. What do they know;'. And he hardly notices the slip in grammar as a repeated groaning starts up from the floor below, loud through the insubstantial floor, and again he feels sickened by this place as he takes another long gulp, glad for the comfort of the drink, before he continues: 'about business; about even their minor rôle through their work, the effect of even their pushing of a button, or putting in of a piece of data; or how they fit into the economy as a whole? They're all such egotists: living for each new billboard, advert – anything that will give them some idea of what to buy next; a slave to commerce. And all this watched over by the politicians, actively facilitated by men deep in the bankers' purses – so deep, that they're in ours. Only capitalism *flourishes in our society, and the people are lulled along, too apathetic to notice, let alone take a stand. No wonder the only words I heard in the office today were between two young ladies discussing the latest of William Gates' ways to swell his fortune: wanting to buy it! Almost every space in the city's centre is covered with some form of advertising – and none question it, for if one feels they can feather their nest a little, then who really cares if we are in truth just slaves with some freedoms?'*

And as he writes the line, the sudden noise of traffic clattering over the little bridge makes him look up, startled into disgust by the noise and the dirt of the modern age. He takes another drink, quickly, and has to pour now for the fifth time as he sees the emptiness of the glass; but he is thankful for the blessing the liquid brings: the numbness, and the thoughts. He glances at the paper, slowly starting to become filled, and his right-hand moves again back to the pen; and as he picks it up, another loud and noisy clatter comes from the bridge behind, sickening him as he starts his work.

'But industry, what is industry but the embodiment of our "progression": a progression towards dirt, depravity and annihilation? The road, what is that but another symbol of humanity's increased ability to destroy our planet, with cars belching out as they do black dirt and smog? Anyone who has been through a town of a night, let alone a city, can't help but have noticed the numbers on the roads, with mad drivers pushing shrieking horns and children knocked down every minute. Again, no one seems to care, always turns a blind eye to these instruments of pain, even when our world is practically

screaming out to us that She is finished. No, all are too caught up in their own affairs, too much hedonists to even think for a moment of what they do, and it is now the case that that extends to every sphere of human life.

'The other day, I was walking through the city centre, scarcely after dark, and there was not a thing there that could go against my view of the degeneracy of the modern age. Even down P--- Street, one of the great streets of commerce, I saw couples, many of them, with their arms around each other in the street, doing more than any decent kiss, and virtually copulating in the street. Is this progress, freedom? Going on from so public a place, my route home takes me to an area where there is "nightlife", and where there are no checks left on even the basest of depravities. On B--- Street, a place has sprung up, and the silhouettes on its outside, right up the walls, are a graphic advert that attests to the debauchery that goes on within. On a main street, even at six, they will turn its lights on, the flashing silhouettes of the dancers, and that is the example we set for our young.' And he clutches his pen tighter as he scratches the characters onto the page, his anger growing now at this crass generation betraying its past. Quickly, he takes another drink and lays the pen down, giving himself over to these thoughts, of bullets and bombs, and then the pain starts to sink in again. Again, he pours himself another dram of the whisky - anything for even a moment's respite - and then he finds the sadness of these thoughts pulling his hand towards the drawer.

Slowly, he pulls it out, the bottom one of that desk, and in it sits a long metal tool: the barrel, and below that the container for the magazine, and the handle with its dark figures; all the dull metal of an old and weathered companion, as much an enemy as a friend. He sits for a few seconds like that, just staring at it, and the sight tortures him just as much as would a long dead friend standing in that room; and for a time he thinks of death before a secondary bang of traffic brings him back to himself, making him turn back in disgust to the words just written on the paper before him. Vacantly, he glares at it, at the still wet ink, and then at long last, picks up his pen and continues to write.

'There was a time when none of that happened, when people respected the world, respected themselves: when did that time go? My God, now'- (and he stops again for another gulp from the glass) 'even the pubs are filled by the same licentiousness; for tonight, like on any other occasion one might try to name, I could hear the sounds of a pair of strangers screaming in each other's ecstasy from one of the cubicles as I dropped in there for some bladder's relief between my drinks. The debauchery is open now, and I shudder to even think about that girl, and that other man, with their faces pressed to the mouth of one of their friends, in both cases of the same sex, doing God knows what with their hands which were down the others' trousers. No, I cannot think of it anymore, for even thinking of the smell of these places, the stale vomit and sweat, makes me feel sick; and the drinking doesn't stay in the pubs. Out in the streets, even, these young people, these "students", stagger around, probably drunk from the night before and yet still up to the same cavorting and brawls the next night and the next.'

And now he drains the last of his glass, glancing up to see the decanter empty, and he lets out a groan at the sight as he places it back down. Momentarily, a part of him thinks of the cabinet behind, and he gets up, scarcely aware that he does so and practically falling with the movement, before he moves quickly to unlatch its door and bring a second back to the desk. Again, he knocks back an immediate glass, hardly even in control of his hand as he moves it to his lips, and as he returns it to the table his eyes rest momentarily on the revolver that lies in that drawer. For a second, he thinks again, and then the draw of the cold barrel, of examining it and the memories, passes again, and he returns the pen to his hand.

'But the decadence refuses to end there: with this "liberty" have come "individual rights", and now the world runs riot in the glory it perceives itself to have attained. Again and again, I hear about children with no respect for their parents, some who even abuse *them*; and then yet others who take the same tone with their teachers, who have hit them, rather than the other way round. That would not even have been possible in our day, nor would it have been accepted; yet now it is never these louts who are blamed, but the parents, others, and the culprits freed from all responsibility.' And here he spits on the ground, struggling not to shake in his anger and even shame at what the world has become. 'And that even extends to the Armed Forces, to the Police; no longer do they feel any debt. Who could seriously want to live in such a distorted, animadvert and heinously unjust place as the world of today? Take the G8 Summit just a *few years ago, or this reaction to the bankers' greed: people seem to believe that Justice should only work one way - their way, and anyone who gets in the way of that, particularly if they try to uphold the law, or simply do their duty, becomes a scapegoat and an enemy; just as hated, another target of the crowds. I have heard people talk, and even these 'students' believe the Army, the Police, simply to be agents whose sole thought is their oppression. My God, never truer has the phrase 'panem et circenses' ever been!'.*

And a tear falls from his eye as the emotion overwhelms him and he lowers his head to his hands.

All this time, he has been sitting at his desk, scratching away with the pen with his right hand and clutching the cup with his left, lifting it now and then to his lips. Again and again, he has topped it up, hardly noticing, and as he has continued he has become steadily more and more drunk, his characters becoming now little more than a messy scrawl on the page; and every few minutes, he has glanced down again towards that drawer.

Now, as he looks again at the page, the lines begin to blur with the tears and the drink, and so he looks up, shaking his head once more as the pen finds itself again laid upon the desk. He looks left and then right, scarcely perceiving the dark window in the dankness of the light, and then his gaze finally lights upon the crystal of this second decanter, and he moves his right hand towards it, his hand gripping it now at the corner of the base. His head lowers slightly, weighed down by the drink, and as he begins to raise the vessel to look at it, his mind returns again to that gun in the drawer; and he lowers his arm slowly to put the decanter back on the desk, his limbs seeming to struggle against him through the haze. Now, he bends his whole body towards the bottom of that desk, his left hand stretched out and reaching for the mental handle of the gun.

Slowly, and with care, he picks it up, straightening, and now he begins to examine it in the light, his brain distractedly captivated at first by the slight reflection of the light on its barrel; and then it begins to dwell on all the places this gun has been, all the lost friends. For a while, he marvels over its contours, at times the physical self almost combining with the reveries of thought as he turns it over, over and back, with the thoughts of his death now far from his mind; and in his state of inebriation he is hardly aware of the action of his fumbling and drunken fingers which contract uncontrollably; while his ears miss the harsh metallic click of the safety catch as they jar it out of position.

It is now, though, as his fingers run over the parts of the gun, that his eyes look up again, seeing how it catches the light, and that his bleary vision notes again in the background the rich crystal shape of the decanter, still upon the desk, and now it is that that holds the entirety of his mind. The guns slips from his mind as his leaden arm lowers to his side, and now his eyes note the emptiness of the decanter, and the absence of more than a few drops of that rich, brown liquid; and now he picks it up again, his right hand clasped around its neck, and he starts to rise. Slowly, he begins to stand, only half-conscious of his drunken instinct to drink more, ever more, as he begins to walk, swaying back and forth, towards the cabinet at the back of the room.

In seconds, he is standing before it, though some part of him wonders how he has got there, and he looks desperately through the glass at the rows of decanters, all filled, which line the shelves; and he stares at them blankly before it finally registers that he will need to open the doors to feel their taste on his tongue. He looks upwards first, and only then does he raise his hands, finally realising that they are full, and so he will need to do something in order to get in. First, he brings the contents of his right hand up towards his face, the decanter, and he is still able to remember why it is there as he lowers the arm down again, thinking what it is he must do. It is then that he feels the weight in his left hand - something metal, and balanced - and he has to raise his hand again, bring it right up to his face, before any part of him can remember what it might be.

He sees its shiny bulk in front of his face, uncomprehending, and now he begins to twist it round, turning it every which way in the desperate hope that it will become clearer, that he will understand what this curious object is; for he has no recollection of taking the gun, that metal instrument of death, away from the table. He looks at it again now, turning it, and suddenly he is looking down its barrel, still without a shred of comprehension, and his fingers have been twitching for an age. It is now, then, that he feels the sweat on his right arm, on the hand, and the decanter starting to slip, moving down slightly, and he squeezes his fingers together, tightening his grip; but fingers squeeze together, unable to stop themselves, on both hands, to tighten around the object which they hold.

It is deafening, thunderous, in the now quiet building- the explosion of that gun as the bullet comes roaring out. To him, it seems bizarre - the silence, and then the gradual loss of perception that seems to take an age, going on beyond anything that the drink could do, and then the juddering fall that seems to last for eternity. Momentarily, only, is he aware of the sound of the gun, and his mind is still unable to grasp what it is that has been in his hand, as it is heard three floors below; and he is oblivious of the descent of the decanter, falling now as his hand loses its grip, and his ears cannot hear its harsh and terrifying crash as it hits the floor, shattering to a thousand shards, even before his body begins its own backward descent to the floor, swaying twice before it begins its slow arc through the air. His mind is gone by the time it makes its heavy thump against its wood; and his breath and heart are stilled but a few seconds later - stilled, as the blood and brains well out from his shattered head to mix with the bright, crystal shards; and the last fiery drops of the liquid that has served as his sustenance for the last two years of his life.

*

It was not until morning that the neighbours phoned the police; they wouldn't let even something like that cheat them of their sleep beyond what the noise had already stolen from them; and then the body was cleaned up, notes taken, and the corpse thrown into the equivalent of a pauper's grave.

To the police, the forensics office, it was obvious: a simple suicide. He had even left a note, for no one at his newspaper knew about the article, nor would anyone have believed that such a bleak piece was meant for them, even if anyone at *The G---* had heard about his death. Besides, there hadn't been any title; and he had never been in the habit of talking to the people at his work. Only one officer thought, just for a second, that it was something else that might have been - a horrific accident, generated by drink, lack of sleep and a mind depressed by its own isolation - but his view was simply blown away by the laughter of every other official to look at the case. There was too much evidence; and so, unfeelingly, and with little ceremony, he was bundled into the ground and his files closed: another victim of the uncaring world.

Charles Eades is currently studying English and Theatre Studies at the University of Warwick. He has one previously published work, a teenage fantasy novel entitled *Son of the Lamp.*, and currently lives in Macclesfield, Cheshire.

Charles Eades has been writing since the age of eight, and **January Brings the Snow** is his first published ghost story, written with inspiration from Edgar Allen Poe, H.P. Lovecraft and any other horror writers he would care to mention.

January Brings the Snow

It was a snowy night in January when I knocked on the door of the cottage. The wind blew hard and the snow fell heavily as I stood outside, shivering. The man who answered it was old and weary; he stared out at me suspiciously before letting me in. His cottage was situated on a hill with a small dark forest behind it and the road had been difficult, so it was with relief that I stepped in from the cold. A fire burned in the kitchen and the old man bade me sit down and brewed me a warm drink. The room was dark but for the fire, and he sat down opposite me as I drank.

'You're not from round here.' said the old man at last.

'That's right,' I replied. He did not seem curious about this and said no more. 'I apologise for disturbing you.' I continued. 'I was on my way to Hampton when I got lost in the snow. The roads are very bad. When I saw your house up here I left the car and came on foot.'

'I understand,' said the old man. 'You're not the first to have been forced to come here by harsh weather. Fortunately Hampton's not far. You can spend the night here and then carry on to the village in the morning.'

'That's very kind of you,' I said. 'Yours is the first house I've seen for miles.'

'It's very remote. We don't usually have snow this bad, but at its worst it can isolate the place for weeks. I don't tend to go out in winter for fear of being unable to get back.'

'You live all on your own out here?'

'Oh yes. There's been no-one else in this house since...' He stopped. 'Well, as you say, I live alone.'

I nodded, wondering what had made him stop. The wind howled down the chimney. The fire crackled in the hearth, casting shadows all around the room. My gaze swept the kitchen, watching the shadows as they danced in the firelight. Out of the corner of my eye I saw something poking out of a cupboard in the corner. Turning towards it, I saw it was a large wooden sledge, but what struck me was that it was pure white, and so shiny as to be almost new.

'That's a fine sledge you've got there.' I commented. The old man saw me looking and eyed the sledge himself.

'Yes,' he said shortly. 'Very fine,'

It occurred to me that the sledge looked as if it had been bought yesterday, yet this man was surely too old to be interested in sledging, and as there were no children here it seemed odd that he should have it with him.

'Whose is it?' I asked, thinking that perhaps it belonged to relatives living elsewhere.

'Mine,' he replied.

'How long have you had it?'

'Ever since I was a child,'

I looked at him questioningly, and then back at the sledge. It was so clean it could have been made barely a week ago, and even if the old man brushed it thoroughly and gave it a fresh lick of paint every day it could not have remained whole and unbroken for such a long time. Not unless it had never been used since its purchase, and even then time and age would have taken the sheen from it and darkened its snow-white colour.

'You are surprised, I see.' said the old man.

I didn't know what to say. 'I must admit it is in very good condition having lasted so long.' I said.

'I have had it a very long time. And over the years it has never lost its colour, or its strength, or its beauty. It is a timeless thing.'

'But how is this possible?'

'I will tell you if you like. But I must warn you, it is not a pleasant story.'

The room seemed to grow colder at his words. I looked him in the eyes. 'Tell me the story.' I said at length.

The old man settled back in his chair. 'I have lived in this house ever since I was twelve years old,' he began. 'My family moved here from the North. We didn't mind living so far from the nearest village, in fact we liked it. The fields and forests to explore were good compensation for the lack of people. However the snow was very different. When it snowed heavily, we had difficulty getting to the village and sometimes we would be snowed in. But the best thing about living on a hill was the sledging. The first time it snowed here my father took me to the village to buy a sledge. In those days all sledges were wooden, not dissimilar to the toboggans they have in America, but far stronger than the shabby plastic things children use nowadays. It was in that shop in Hampton that I first found it.' The old man indicated the sledge in the corner.

'It was the colour that attracted me. Not just the dull ivory you find on some wooden sledges but a proper white that gleamed in the sun. I begged my father to buy it and when we went home, me pulling it along behind us, I felt proud showing it off to the other children with their own, rather less impressive sledges. I had a brother and sister then, both of whom like me were eager to try it out immediately. Our parents said it was too late at night and we would have to wait until morning. The sledge was left outside, and it started to snow. Before I got into bed I went and looked out of my window. I could see the sledge in the yard, dimly amongst the falling snow. I was about to get back into bed when I saw something very strange.

'There was a little girl sitting on the sledge. I hadn't seen her arrive, it was as if she had materialised out of the snowfall. Her hair was white as the snow around her and she was dressed only in what looked like a school uniform. I remember thinking she must have been freezing, but she didn't shiver or look uncomfortable, though she was very pale. My mother came in at that point and when I looked back at the sledge, the girl was gone.'

The old man stopped.

'A girl?' I said. 'Are you sure you didn't dream it?'

'Positive,' replied the old man. 'I saw her as clearly as I see you. A pale girl of about nine or ten with wispy white hair.'

'What if she was just an ordinary child, who had got lost?'

'She would have knocked at the house then, wouldn't she? Besides, no ordinary girl could have sat so still in the freezing cold. She sat still as a statue, staring into the distance. It wasn't the last time I saw her either.'

'You saw her again?'

'Yes. The very next day. That morning we went sledging, my brother and sister and I. It had stopped snowing and seemed a good day for it. That sledge was the only one we had, so we had to take turns on it. My sister got the first go, on account of being the eldest. She got on the sledge and prepared to set off. That was when I saw *her* again. She stood a little distance away from us, watching. The night before I had seen her at an angle and she had been facing away from me. This time I saw her face.' The old man shuddered. 'It was the most chilling thing I've ever seen in my life. She watched us with an expression of such malevolence that I could barely look at her. She met my gaze for a moment, and there was something in her eyes besides the hatred. It looked like anticipation. Or hunger. Then she looked away from me to where my sister was sitting on the sledge, in the exact position that the little girl had been the night before. My sister started down the hill, and the girl followed her with those horrible eyes, and an awful feeling of dread came over me. I turned away from the girl and ran towards my sister, shouting a warning. I was too late. I watched the sledge pick up speed, carrying her away faster and faster, until it seemed to veer out of control. It was winding an erratic, unstoppable path down the hill, and my sister was struggling to hold on. Then she crashed into a tree.'

The old man paused for a moment, clearly shaken by the memory. 'She broke her neck and was killed instantly. But the sledge was miraculously unharmed. After it happened I stood there at the top of the hill, staring down at where she lay. My brother was screaming, he ran inside to get our parents, but I just stood there. I looked back at where the girl had been, but she was gone.

'There was no more sledging at our house for a long time after that. My parents wouldn't have let us even if we wanted to, and I had other reasons. I was now quite certain that the girl was somehow controlling the sledge, and that she had made it kill my sister. But I didn't tell my parents this, and I didn't know what to do about it. However, I thought that as long as no-one used the sledge then everything would be fine.

'A year passed. Christmas came without incident, but January and the New Year brought a fresh fall of snow, even heavier than the previous year. Although we never went sledging anymore, we still used the sledge occasionally. In particular, when I and my brother went into the village, while the snow was down we would take the sledge with us as a form of transport. We would take turns riding on it whilst the other pulled it along. One day we were in the village doing this when we realised it was getting late. Our parents wanted us home by five due to it getting dark earlier, so we got on a bus that would take us to a bus stop near our house. Dragging a sledge onto a bus was not an easy task but we managed nonetheless. But during the journey a creeping sense of unease came upon me. I looked around the bus. Outside it was not dark yet, and there were only a few other passengers. Yet as I sat there the noise of the engine fell strangely silent. We were still moving but there was no noise inside or outside. Then the windows of the bus began to mist over and the lights went out, plunging the vehicle into darkness.

'Panic set in. Some of the other passengers were screaming. The driver could not see; he was fighting to keep control of the bus. I got out of my seat; I was too frightened to sit still. I stumbled out into the aisle and then stopped in my tracks. The little pale girl stood directly before me, she was so close that I could touch her. She smiled malignantly, her eyes like knives piercing me. Then there was a moment of pure chaos and I blacked out.'

The old man stopped again. I noticed the fire was burning low. I reached down and loaded some more coal on, then sat back and waited for him to continue.

'I woke up in a hospital bed,' said the old man. 'The bus had crashed of course. Most of us escaped with cuts and bruises, myself included, but there was one casualty.'

'Your brother?' I said hesitantly.

He nodded. 'The sledge once more remained intact, but it had served its purpose. It was clear to me now that we didn't need to ride the sledge in order for bad things to happen. The girl, who or whatever she was, was more powerful than that.'

'Why did you not destroy it?' I asked.

'I thought about doing that. I wondered if it would work. But that theory was proved wrong in dreadful circumstances.

'When he saw my brother's body, my father went mad. At first he was inconsolable, weeping bitterly for hours on end, then he flew into a rage that lasted days, and nothing me or my mother could do would calm him down. Then a week after the accident, he went outside and saw the sledge sitting in the yard. He began to rage and scream at it, claiming that all the trouble had started when we bought it, convinced that it had something to do with everything. I watched from the window as my father built up a large fire and lit it, waiting until it was at full blaze. Then he took the sledge in his arms and hurled it into the fire.

'The explosion nearly blinded me. When my vision was recovered, I looked out once more and saw the yard was littered with patches of flames and debris, whilst in the middle of it all sat the sledge, upright and intact as ever. But amongst the burning piles I saw to my horror the charred body of my father, still aflame. And in the smoke stood the girl, glaring at my father's corpse with all her hatred.

'I never touched the sledge after that. But I was still desperate to find out the reason for all this misfortune, or at least find a way to put a stop to it. I thought about telling the village priest and asking him to exorcise a sledge, until I realised how silly that sounded. So instead I went to the library. They had a section in which old newspapers were kept, with some dating back fifty years. I had never been interested in such things but now I looked for something, anything that might explain these events. At last I discovered an article that told me at least half the story. I still have it with me.'

The old man fished in his pocket and produced a faded piece of newspaper which he handed to me. It was dated in the 1920s and had a headline that read "Father convicted of murdering daughter". I read on. The article described a particularly unpleasant incident. The father in question had apparently been sledging with his ten-year-old daughter, and he had deliberately pushed her, whilst she was on the sledge, into a pond. The little girl had drowned there. On the page was a black-and-white photograph of the dead girl, smiling sweetly at the camera. She had been a pretty child. I showed it to the old man.

'Is this the girl you saw?' I asked.

He nodded. 'I'd know that face anywhere. Of course she was far less happy when I saw her. I asked some of the villagers about the incident. A few of them had been alive when it happened, and I gathered that the convicted man had been an abusive father, prone to heavy drinking and violence. His wife had died in suspicious circumstances but there hadn't been enough evidence for a conviction. But when the little girl was killed there were witnesses who swore it was deliberate. No-one knew why he murdered her. He was drunk, or mad, or maybe just evil. Whatever the reason, it was a terrible thing and I believed then it was the cause of all our miseries. I was convinced the sledge sitting in the corner was the same sledge the girl had been riding when she drowned in the pond. I went back to the man who sold us the sledge, and though he wasn't sure, he said he had owned it a long time, possibly since the date of the girl's death. I offered to sell it back to him but he had heard what happened to my sister, and though he didn't say so, I knew he didn't want something in his shop with such a grisly record.

'I now believed that the sledge was being haunted by the little girl who died on it, and that she was controlling it and using it to do terrible things. I didn't know how she kept it in prime condition or how she was able to crash the bus, but I knew it was her.'

'But why?' I said. 'If it was her father who killed her, what could she have had against you?'

'I don't know,' said the old man. 'But her father was dead when we got the sledge. I think perhaps our using it somehow awakened her, and all the hatred and misery caused by her father was being directed at us. I think if it had been some other family she would have done the same.'

'So what did you do?'

'I knew I couldn't destroy the sledge, and asking a priest about it would probably have got me thrown out of the church. So I went home and locked the sledge in the cellar and swore never to let it see daylight again.

'For years it remained down there. My mother faded with age and sorrow and by the time I left home she was dead. I left the sledge behind. I hoped no-one would find it, and if they did I hoped they would be able to get rid of it forever. Years passed. I got a job, got married, and we had a baby. But then my job in London was made redundant and money grew scarce. We could no longer afford to live in the city. The only other place for us to go was here. No-one had lived in it since my mother died and I still had a legal claim to it.

We moved down here and got new jobs. But I hadn't forgotten the sledge. I didn't dare look in the cellar for fear I would find it there, or worse, I would find the girl. That winter we had our first Christmas here. Then in January it snowed again. My wife, unlike me, was still fond of sledging and she decided to take our two-year-old son out. I went with them for her sake, though I knew I didn't dare ride a sledge myself. My childhood experiences had instilled in me a lifelong fear of sledging.

'In the village there's a large pond. Sometimes in the winter it freezes so hard that it's safe to go skating on it. My wife suggested we take our plastic sledges down there and have a skate on the pond. We both had skates and my wife intended to pull our son on the sledge over the ice. So we went down there and my wife skated along with our son in tow. I stood on the bank, happy to watch them, but not quite ready to join in.

'It was then that I saw *her.* She stood at the edge of the pond watching my wife and son with the same malevolence I had seen as my sister rode the sledge all those years ago. She looked at me once more and I realised with horror that this was the very pond in which she had drowned. I cried out to my wife, making to run towards them. Once again, I was too late. With a sound like a gunshot the ice split apart beneath my wife's feet and she plunged into the water, pulling my son's little sledge with her. They disappeared without a sound. The next few moments were like a dream. I stood immobile, hearing only dimly the shouts around me, saw through a haze people running to help, crawling across the ice, plunging their hands into the water. Less than an hour later, their bodies were laid out on the snow. I stroked my wife's wet hair, kissed my son's cold forehead, and then made my way home, all alone.'

There was silence. The old man stared into the fire, now burning very low indeed. I watched him, too appalled to speak.

'When I got home I went straight to the cellar,' the old man continued. 'The sledge was still there. Of course it was still there. I got it out and set it in that cupboard, and it's been there ever since.'

I realised my drink had gone cold, but I clutched it just the same. Despite the warmth of the room, I was shivering. 'And the girl?' I said. 'Have you seen her since then?'

'No,' replied the old man. 'But I feel her presence always. She doesn't just haunt the sledge, she haunts the house now. I believe the sledge was only ever a tool of hers; it was a doorway through which she could enter our lives and exact her revenge. Her power is such that the sledge isn't the only thing she can control: she crashed the bus, she made the fire explode, and she cracked the ice.'

'But why did she not kill you like your family?'

'Oh she will. I'm certain now that she will. She is simply biding her time. I think I was saved until last because I chose the sledge in the first place. However, I do not think I will be spared.'

'Then why don't you run? Why do you stay here?'

'Because she will find me. My leaving here might delay her but it won't stop her. She will always find me and at the first chance, she will end it.'

I was about to say something else when we heard a knocking at the door. One, two, three. One, two, three. The knocking persisted in a continuing cycle. We both froze and listened.

'Who on earth could that be?' I said. I got up to answer it but he grabbed me, his eyes suddenly wide with fear. 'Don't!' he cried. 'It's *her*! Listen!'

I listened, and sure enough, above the knocking at the door and the howling of the wind outside, I heard the faint sound of a child's voice singing a nursery rhyme:

'Oranges and lemons, say the bells of St Clements,

I owe you five farthings, say the bells of St Martins...'

Something about the voice, which tinkled like a bell, filled me with dread, and we stood there, the old man and I, huddled in the firelight while the noise persisted outside. Then the knocking stopped and the wind fell silent. But the voice, rising now until it sounded as if it were right at the door, continued vigorously.

'Here comes the candle to light you to bed,

Here comes the chopper to chop off your head...'

'She's come for me,' moaned the old man. 'She's come for me!' He crouched down by the fire, moaning piteously.

I looked at him helplessly, and then jumped as the knocking commenced once more, now louder and more persistent than ever. One two three one two three one two three. Hesitantly, I stepped out into the darkened hallway. As the knocking continued, I walked forward towards the door. I didn't know what I would find there, or what I would do, but I knew the old man was in dreadful danger, and I wasn't going to let the evil thing outside take him without a fight. It never occurred to me that I might share his fate.

With a shaking hand, I reached out and clasped the door handle. The knocking reached a crescendo and I swung open the door. A blast of cold wind, solid as a wall, struck me and threw me to the floor. I felt cold hands around my throat and two demonic eyes stared at me through a mask of hatred. I writhed on the floor as the evil fingers dug into my neck. Then it passed and I was able to breathe again, but as I choked and gasped there came a terrible scream from the kitchen. I got to my feet and staggered through the hall.

The kitchen was empty. The fire had gone out and the wind outside had been silenced. I looked down and saw the old man on the floor. He was still; eyes open, cold and lifeless. I crouched down and put my hand on his chest. His heart had stopped. For a moment, out of the silence of the night I heard the light, tinkling laughter of a delighted little girl. Then there was nothing.

Richard Willis first started writing from the age of 7, when he would scribble away for hours in a red folder filled with lined paper. Since then, he has attained a BA Honours degree in English Literature at the University of Worcester, and written several novels, as well as countless short stories. One of these novels, *Alternate*, is already available as a Kindle eBook, and a second novel, *Familiar Strangers*, will also be available through Kindle soon enough.

Richard Willis is an avid reader of myths, lore, history, Edgar Allan Poe and H. P. Lovecraft, which all provide inspiration to incorporate both mystery and mayhem into his stories. It has always been Richard's ambition to have his writings published and stand alongside his favourite authors, his peers... and rivals.

Hereditary Instinct

"Why do I want to win?

Because I don't want to lose!"

A deep gasp sounded as Anna Weathers forced herself awake. Those prominent words echoed from a fleeting dream and screamed with the loudest sound. The voice was familiar with a commanding tone and lessons to teach but the speaker was elusive and hid from Anna's waking mind.

Sound and sunlight burst in with a single shot and she awoke with a sudden jolt.

Cold metal pressed against her face as the world slipped into focus. She lay in the back of a truck, huddled in an uncomfortable heap with her weight pressing hard against the rigid floor. The tyres of the old truck dipped and bounced as it pushed an even thirty along a dirt track, shaking the trailer. The joints of the aging beast creaked with every bump as the rough terrain tested the seasoned metal.

She had no idea where she was or how she got there. Flashes of memory barged through the delirium and gripped Anna tight with reality's cold fingers. She had no defence against the push and surrendered as the splintered moments bullied and harassed her.

Someone was stood behind her.

A stranger with his face reflected on the glass.

An attack. Shooting pain. Then, blackness.

Those few images seared her mind's eye but were the extent of her recollection. She couldn't see any further, her head felt heavy and despite the sudden start her eyes begged to close again. A blight flowed through her veins, trying to steal her eyes and send her back to that oppressive murk. She could feel it trudging through her blood turning the world to a blackened tar while she lay helpless.

"Time is money."

The voice returned to churn the wheels.

Anna tried to move. Mobility slowly crept back into her legs but her arms were held still. She wasn't to blame for her frailty, someone had bound her hands.

She looked down into her cradled lap and saw the distinct green, plastic tie wrapped around her wrists, holding them together.

A stampede of questions bounced off whatever memories she could scrape together.

What happened?

Where was she?

Who'd done this?

The cries sounded but there was no response. The blight in her veins hazed those vital clues, keeping them poised on the tip of her tongue.

Persistence prompted a search for alternative stimuli. She needed more information, anything she could hold onto to piece together what happened.

Trapped inside its belly, Anna studied the confines of the trailer. It was an old army surplus wagon, with faded green paint and weathered metal. The trailer was spacious and covered by an arched tarp roof which stretched from one side to the other.

The air inside smelt musty and stirred memories of camping with her family as a child. This nostalgia had no place inside the beast but she kept it close regardless. For a reason she couldn't explain the memories worked to replace the blight by encouraging that familiar voice to return. The identity was still lost but it was welcomed.

"Dream as if you'll live forever.

Live as if you'll die today."

The voice spoke aloud and the words resonated with a growing clarity. She recognised each phrase as a prompt from her slumbering past as they slowly returned to their rightful place ahead of the pack.

A guardian was watching over her.

The truck shuddered as it ran across another untamed breach in the road. Anna rolled from side to side in the commotion until she eventually came to rest back in her original groove.

As she nestled down, a liquid trickled along the indented floor and touched her cheek. It felt warm and viscous against her skin, but she couldn't see where it was coming from.

Another unexpected bump forced her head down and pushed her back into the liquid. The resulting splash tossed some of it into her mouth. It had an instant bitter taste against her tongue which made her gag as she quickly spat it out. There was a metallic tang, copper, and there was a familiarity to it that she just couldn't place. Whatever it was, it scared her, the taste and the texture was repulsive and in response triggered a new and welcomed stir.

She gave a stern push with her shoulder and nudged himself away from the floor. A slight roll onto her backside and a strained lower back took her the rest of the way and she sat up straight.

Immediately, the need to know pestered for answers again, and Anna obliged.

She looked into the back of the trailer. Two rusted tool cases lined the left side while a pile of rolled up blankets lay bundled to the right.

Her wandering sight then latched onto a new spectacle.

There was someone else in the trailer with her.

With her back turned and a frantic panic pulling her in every direction; Anna simply hadn't noticed her at first.

The fellow passenger lay on her back. She was dressed in blue jeans and a white jumper with long blonde hair tied into a ponytail. Anna didn't recognise her.

Her eyes were open but she wasn't moving,

"Hey! Are you okay?" Anna asked.

No reply.

Anna noticed the wound. A small tear down the left side of her neck was held in contrast against the girl's pale skin. The wound was only a few centimetres in length but it had been enough to kill her and the purged crimson now lined the floor.

The liquid on her cheek, the copper on her tongue, Anna followed the long trail of red to her knees and could finally give the metallic tang a name. The pit already in her stomach opened wider to swallow the dread now inspired.

Her sight drifted back to the girl and she noticed a thin slither of metal sticking out of her throat.

It was a needle.

A clue!

This first piece of the puzzle pushed those stubborn memories off her tongue and sent them clambering into order.

Someone was stood behind her.

A stranger. An attack.

No! Further back than that.

Her 11 O'clock appointment.

Memories came rushing in relentless waves. Anna sifted through them and carefully put them back into ascending order to retell those final hours.

A brunch meeting with a prospective client.

She snapped out of the recollection and looked at his clothes. She was still wearing her blue-grey trouser suit.

The timeline slid into place and she returned to the start.

The meeting had gone well.

She had...

"Hit the ground running."

"Turnover is vanity. Profit is reality."

This was a very important client and she didn't stop until there was a smile on their face and a yes from their mouths.

Recollection dwindled at this point.

There were a few brief flashes.

Difficult to hold.

Two maybe three seconds worth.

She remembered walking back to her car at a local multi-storey. As she neared her BMW she dipped her hand into her handbag to fish out her keys and stopped at the door.

She looked at her own reflection against the driver's side window. One second she was alone basking in her proud smile, the next, someone was stood behind her.

A tall man. The stranger.

He had a thick full beard and wore plane, green army fatigues. A sign of the man he was. The training. His ability.

The memory twisted and stretched.

A run of colours washed the image as a pain pierced her neck.

A compound, the blight.

A hypodermic needle.

Then, blackness.

The memory dispelled any remaining doubt. The stranger – the Hunter – had seen her, tracked her and then attacked with a sedative and swift reflexes.

Who was he?

What did the Hunter want?

Her faculties scurried back into their restored precision and fired assumptions in random bursts.

Keep it quick. Keep it simple.

"Compartmentalise", just like she'd been taught.

The girl was dead. Had been for a while. She's bled out, indicating the time separating the girl's death and her own capture.

Logic stepped in to give the most plausible scenario.

An accident.

The hunter stalked and pounced. A complication. The girl struggled. The needle broke, tearing an artery.

The next question was the most difficult to answer because it ushered in the possibilities of what might lay ahead.

Why was she still alive?

The Hunter, unsatisfied, moved on to the next target and Anna was a happy fit.

The injected fluid wasn't lethal. Meant to subdue, not to kill. The Hunter had bigger plans. A private place. A quiet place. Somewhere he could take his time and savour the kill.

Why was she awake?

The Hunter only brought one dose. Improvised. Not enough sedative to do the job.

That was all Anna needed. It was dumb luck that had given her this reprieve but she took it regardless.

Nothing else for it. All the answers and the conjecture in the world couldn't help her; the only recourse was to escape. She couldn't wait for the truck to stop, she was in no state to fight, she had to get out now and run for her life.

With a rickety balance Anna climbed to her feet and carefully edged to the back of the trailer.

The tarp flaps were loose and open but she couldn't see far beyond the strict confines.

Below was the old dirt road.

To the right was a tall, untamed hedge, baring any further ingress. To the left was a small embankment which dropped into a steep slope and led down to a river.

Above, Anna saw the azure of a clear, blue sky. The ambivalence wasn't lost on her.

She didn't recognise the road. There were no landmarks and the more refined details were locked away behind the hedge and hill. She was far from home, that much was obvious. She was a city girl, born and bread, and these weren't *her* usual hunting grounds.

The truck was only travelling at thirty miles per hour and it was a mere half metre drop to the ground. It would be a simple jump to begin her escape but the inherent danger of what was asked of her made the ground rush by in a dazzling haze.

"You're disappointed if you fail, but you're doomed if you never try."

Wise words pushed themselves to the front of the uncertainty and the risk, announced by that familiar voice.

She recognised the announcer. The doggedness of the uttered prompts finally gave Anna the name as the blight drifted from her blood. It was her Father/Boss. It was his voice that spoke aloud in Anna's mind, daring her to move forward.

Crisis dwelled and nothing could have prepared her for this. No experience and no theory bore the same intensity as being caught in the glare of a Hunter and in the murk Anna latched on to the most potent sound.

Every other credence she could claim to hold scattered in the wind but the fabled words of her Father/Boss remained at the forefront. They were her only life line. Every other thought and every other fortitude had turned to black.

The phrases were motivational thinking passed down from Parent to child, from Parent to child.

Shades of grey down the hereditary line. Birds flying south. A spider's web.

Anna's Father/Boss was from a bygone era and taught his daughter a trade, that's how he loved.

Most kids had a lot less and a lot worse.

The words taught Anna to strive, to stand and take what she deserved. They were never designed for such barbarity but they were all she had. The recourse of the desperate at its most potent.

"No one knows what they can do, until they try."

More words poured to the surface encouraging her survival. She braced herself to jump.

From all the experiences, all the ideas and all the notions that piled in and ran through a single existence, this was the one redeeming aspect that held her steady.

Time to use it.

"We lead with need."

Anna leapt from the truck.

The fall was a swift drop, barely registered. Her feet touched the ground and her gathered speed sent her tumbling over onto her side. With her hands bound Anna could do nothing to control her landing and reluctantly surrendered to the momentum.

The uneven ground slammed and smashed her helpless body with the same cruelty it had inflicted upon the old truck. The world span in an abstract swirl and Anna rolled over and over. Her legs waved free in the calamity while her shoulders took the full brunt of the collision.

A slam onto her right side brought Anna to a sudden stop.

She lay still to collect herself and suffered the shooting pains screaming from head to toe.

"Nothing like biting off more than you can chew and chewing anyway."

More words came to lift her body and keep her moving.

This wasn't over, that was just the first step. No place for sympathy. No time for tears.

Pushing the bruises and scratches aside, she picked herself up.

Anna slipped off her heeled shoes and jogged down the slopping hill. With her hands bound her balance swayed and shifted with every step. She tried to compensate by bobbing her head and swinging her shoulders while she strained her legs to correct any drift.

The crow stride took her to the riverbank where she quickly turned to her left and dashed towards a small cluster of shrubs and bushes.

A place to hide.

This simple plan became her only priority until an unwanted sound spirited her attention away from the trail.

Screeching breaks echoed above her panting breaths and patter of bare feet as the truck came to a sliding halt.

No question, she'd been spotted.

Thoughts of recapture held Anna's attention and in this unexpected lapse she lost her footing.

Her next proceeding step hit the side of a pothole and broke her stride. She toppled over and landed face down in the mud. Momentum threw her into the cold sludge and splashed her across the face and stained her clothes.

Sounds were broadcast on high volume in the secluded fields and beyond her laboured trudge Anna heard the driver's side door slam shut.

She pushed away her own calamity; the Hunter was on the prowl.

Anna's first impulse was to lie still. She would gladly hide amongst the thickets and accept her role as prey if it meant she could escape.

The Hunter stood on the verge, scouring the grounds below.

Sharpened instincts.

Predatory.

He knew the land. The best places to hide. The pathways and the worn trails.

He could always spot the deer with the limp.

No time to pray.

The search was over.

Anna had used up all of her luck for that day.

Holding both sight and scent the Hunter galloped down the hill with swift, bold strides.

Anna picked herself up out of the mud and turned from her pursuer.

"Don't compromise yourself.

You're all you've got."

She couldn't allow a few aches and pains to lull her into surrender. She couldn't get captured again!

"The three ingredients.

Learning, earning and yearning."

She didn't care about the Hunter's name, or what would be gained from all this. All that preoccupied Anna was staying out of the net; every other concern was changed to second and third.

Anna didn't turn around; her sight remained fixed to the ragged trail along the riverbank. She could hear a thunder of hooves behind her as heavy army boots pounded the soft grass with a relentless stampede. The Hunter was closing in. The restricting path kept Anna pinned into a straight line, her legs churned through the aches and bruises but she couldn't run fast enough and there was no way to shake her pursuer.

Two firm hands shoved her back.

The sudden knock sent Anna tumbling into the river.

First there was a rush of air and then an explosion of icy water.

She couldn't breathe.

Streams of water rushed up into her nose and she choked on the invading substance. Panic swept in to replace her most recent guile and she kicked and fought to stay above the water.

She couldn't stop. She couldn't get caught!

"Quitting wrinkles the soul."

She flipped onto her side and sat up in the water.

A fresh new breath filled her lungs as she gasped in the open air.

Her rallied spirit met its rival and before she could react, the Hunter bore down on top of her.

Two firm hands held Anna's shoulders and pushed her back under the water.

"Nihil Obstat;

Nothing stands in the way."

Instinct governed again. In response Anna lifted her right leg and before it was spotted she drove it hard into the Hunter's gut.

The swift kick left the Hunter winded and he fell away, releasing Anna from his grasp.

A chance. Anna took it.

She lifted himself out of the water and climbed back to her feet. The water was shallow so close to the shore, and she waded through with relative ease.

She left the Hunter gasping for air and continued to race along the riverbank.

Anna tried to hold a single strategy, but she found herself divided between her course and the danger still lingering behind her. Self preservation demanded that she kept her sight trained on the path ahead, but she couldn't help but glance over her shoulder.

The Hunter had caught his breath and was back on his feet. The kick had winded him but he'd managed to shake it off and climbed out of the river.

Anna returned to the trail. Where was she going? Over the river there was nothing but lonely roads and empty farm land. In the distance she could just make out the smudged contours of a few houses but they had to be over five miles away, maybe more.

She looked back.

The Hunter had almost caught up. The altercation had slowed his pace, but only by a little. Anna noticed he was carrying a long, thick branch that he'd found amongst the trees and shrubs. The wood had faded to a pale white but it looked sturdy enough.

Anna turned to the trail.

Where could she go? What could she do? The whole world shrank to a single trail and a deep and fast flowing river.

Had to keep running.

Had to escape!

She looked back one more time.

The hunter had caught up with her. He'd already drawn back the branch with a firm lean and was ready to swing.

Anna returned to the trail. Maybe she could...

The Hunter swung the bat.

The lump of wood made contact with the back of Anna's head. A dense thud against flesh and bone ended her flee with a blunt snap.

Pain faded into delirium and a ringing in her ears.

The strings were cut clean away from her arms and legs and she plunged into a crumpled heap. Consciousness shifted to a drifting ghost and all she had was a sideways view of the world with no way to change it.

The Hunter loomed over his subdued prey. The pain in his gut boiled to anger and he drew a knife from the sheath attached to his belt.

The blade gleamed and held Anna's sight as he moved it down to her throat. Her blood raced but she couldn't scream and she couldn't move, all Anna could do was to lie there delirious and watch from the back seat.

The knife fell out of view while decisions were made without her say-so.

The Hunter contemplated ending the game. Things had gotten out of hand and the spoils were almost ruined. He wanted to hurt the deer for what it had done. He wanted to stick it with the knife and make it kick and struggle. It was tempting, very tempting, but an admission stayed his hand. He tapped the knife against his chin and pondered for a moment. He couldn't deny that he was tantalised by the vigour of the game. He hadn't felt his heart race like this for quite some time.

'Patience,' he told himself.

'Take it back. Everything is set up. Why deny yourself? Already had one disappointment today.'

No time to waste. He had to make this quick. They were in the middle of nowhere, but random chance was a bitch.

The Hunter slid the knife back into its sheath and knelt down next to the deer. With a firm grasp he hauled his game over his shoulder and stood up.

Anna dangled limp over her captor. She lifted her head and watched the open trail drift out of sight behind the wild grass. Sensation slowly crept into both faculty and function but what use was it. She couldn't fight him and there was nowhere to run.

Must be a way.

She didn't want to die.

Had to find a way.

"Fail to prepare – prepare to fail!"

The answer fell into view.

The knife.

Anna looked down at the blade; it was within arms' reach.

The Hunter wasn't sloppy; she'd just played dead a little too well.

The knife was there, all she had to do was take it.

Kill.

It was the only way out of all this. He wasn't going to just stop.

Kill!

"Success doesn't come to you.

You go for it."

So go for it!

Her Father/Boss gave the order and she obeyed.

Anna reached down and pulled the knife from its sheath. With a quick, jerked motion she rammed the tip of the blade into the Hunter's back.

The jagged pain made the Hunter's knees buckle and he collapsed onto the ground.

Anna was caught in the flow and toppled down beside him. She held the knife with both bound hands and sat up.

The Hunter was wounded but far from beaten.

In that deciding moment Anna had hesitated. She was no murderer; this wasn't a switch that could just be flicked. She'd held back and only pushed the blade in an inch or two.

It wasn't enough.

"The only failure in life is a failure to try."

'I want to go home! I don't want to die!' Her own voice took the reins.

The Hunter climbed to his feet with a fevered grunt. Snarling teeth and a wild stare were his words of outrage for the offence and a decree of retribution.

Anna held the knife out in front of her, poised and ready.

"No one drowned in their own sweat."

The Hunter charged.

Reaction gave the command and Anna lunged forward with a desperate cry. With all of her weight behind the attack she shoved the knife into the Hunter's chest and drove it hard.

The Hunter took the brunt with a seasoned grit but the sharp blade buried in his stomach sapped his body of vigour and forced him back.

Anna stopped in her tracks and watched as the Hunter plunged into the lapping waters of the river below.

The wound wasn't instantly fatal. Anna stood on the riverbank and stared at the Hunter, counting his shortening breaths as the waters reddened.

She looked down at the knife in her hands and the blood on the blade. She came to a stop, the first since her eyes opened in the back of the old truck. In the direst circumstances the blessings of her Father/Boss had kept her alive. The words had been passed down in the blood and became a spark to keep her heart beating.

Anna Weathers stood on the riverbank and took stock.

There was no hatred; it had just been another obstacle.

There was no taste for it; it was just something she had to do.

She'd survived. This was *her* win.

"I am the master of my fate.

I am the captain of my soul."

J (Julia) Lacey Brooke was born in 1956 in a country village in Leicestershire where she rode horses, taught herself to type and wrote stories. After working for BBC local radio and an advertising agency, she read English Literature and Renaissance History at UEA. She taught English for many years in London and the Southwest, and took a part-time M.Litt at the University of Birmingham's Shakespeare Institute. In 2001, she moved to Sicily to teach MCAS in Syracuse. Widowed and based in rural Tuscany, with a son living in England, she enjoys music, gardening, wildlife and teaching part-time- lecturing on Shakespeare's Italian influences amongst other things- and writes.

Her first novel, *The Mischief Maker, or the Loathsome History of a Malcontent,* the picaresque tragicomedy of a modern revenger spanning 40 years, a great many locations & milieu, was Bookblast's 'book of the month' in December 2011. Her second novel, *Circled By The Sands*, is a darkly hilarious tale set in and out of ex-pat Italy. 'The Haunting of Daisy Thompson' is part of a new collection, *Behind the Pleasance & Other Tales*. She has a new novel, *Hostages to Fortune*, under construction, and you can visit her Author Page on Amazon's Author Central, or via Linkedin.

The Haunting of Daisy Thompson

Everybody agrees that Daisy Thompson has not been herself since her mother died, but it all began a long time before that, on the very day, in fact, that Dr Mahmood had explained that poor Mrs Thompson would probably never recognize anyone again. The medication had simply staved off the inevitable. Fairview would continue to make her as comfortable as possible. She was in no obvious distress. No – Dr Mahmood shook his head – no, there was no possibility of Daisy's mother recovering her faculties. If Daisy would like some family support counselling, Dr Mahmood would happily arrange it…

Daisy was not especially remarkable. She had enough personal eccentricities for Cheney Magna where eccentricity of one sort or another was the norm. Never exactly pretty, she had always looked young for her age: indeed with her button nose and wide-set blue eyes, she resembled nothing so much as a middle-aged Cabbage Patch doll. If she could alter one thing about her appearance, it would be the acquisition of cheekbones, but this was always said as a little joke at her own expense, and at fifty, she was balanced, self-accepting and independent. Daisy's little High Street shop, 'Five A Day', sold locally-produced fruit, vegetables and free-range eggs, and provided Daisy with a daily social life. She sat on the Committee that organized the Summer Fayre, was a valuable member of 'Businesses for Environment' and a volunteer for the Shop-Mobility rota. Childless and eminently responsible, she was often roped in to child-mind for her friends with young families. She visited old Mrs Spears when almost no one else would. If Mrs Spears was not *exactly* a Fascist, her rants were pretty strong stuff – but the poor old duck couldn't help it. The pain of the arthritis was cruel.

Daisy lived above the shop, alone apart from her Labrador Groucho, but she was not lonely. If there had been speculation about Daisy's sex-life – it was said there had been a proper relationship once – this had long since ceased to pre-occupy anyone. Daisy was just Daisy: good-humoured, capable, and obviously *not* sour or nursing a broken heart. Even her best friend, Alice, had stopped trying to fix her up. The truth was that Daisy simply was not interested in intimate physical contact. There had been no childhood trauma. No one had abused her. She had not wanted to be a boy, and she had not had secret, anguishing crushes on girls. There had indeed been one 'boy and girl' affair, as her mother had called it, when Daisy was eighteen and when all her friends were seeing boys, thinking about boys... but Daisy's chief memory of that camping holiday near Totnes with Joe, Daisy curious to know what 'all the fuss was about'– was that sex, and the 'fuss', was vastly overrated.

She'd 'done it', and that might as well be it, as far as Daisy was concerned. Joe had begun dating her friend Sarah and she wished them nothing but well. She was far from being a prude, either – indeed there was nothing prissy about her at all. She was sympathetic to romance, and had a passion for Jane Austen. She simply had no interest in 'romance' that went beyond an eighteenth century drawing room.

She had googled 'Alzheimer's Disease', and became convinced that the doctor was right. These things had to be faced. Really, Mum had stopped being 'Mum' a long time ago. Daisy had adjusted. The main thing now was to make sure that the old lady had all the care she needed, and to hope – Daisy hoped this didn't sound too dreadful – that the end would not be very long. "Unpredictable at this stage," the doctor had said.

The bell rang, and Groucho barked, and padded after Daisy

down the stairs. Alice. "*Daisy!* Is everything okay? I've been thinking and thinking of you today... I'm just picking up Jared, so I can't stop. The Three Bears later? Bryn'll have the kids. We can have a good chat." Dear, kind Alice! But there wasn't much to say.

The pub was cheerfully rowdy, and Daisy and Alice found a corner of a table where they could speak without shouting and drank the local cider. "Poor Daisy," Alice was saying. "It can't have been easy, you poor love. You will tell us if there's anything we can do, anything at all..." Alice's big, bovine eyes misted a little. Her own mother had died the year before.

"I'm fine, honestly, Alice," said Daisy. "It's not a shock. I'm more relieved to, well, to *know*..." Alice's brother Bill joined them. "I'd forgotten it was a Woollybacks night," Alice said. Bill said, "You going to stay? Sing a number for us, Daisy?" So Daisy and Alice watched Bill and the band – a guitar, a violin and a set of drums – fix up the little PA system in the corner, and strike up its familiar medley of folk standards and country and western. After another pint of cider, Daisy got up and sang 'The Sailor Lad', and then, in close harmony with Bill, 'Together Again'. People clapped warmly. "You ought to sing more, Daisy," said Alice when Daisy sat down. The band took a pause, and Bill ordered a round. "Thanks, Bill. Just a half of Rowan's... Oh, all right. A pint."

"You've had quite enough, Marguerite," said a voice distinctly into a small silence. Daisy stared, shook her head. "It's high time you went home."

"Daisy? You okay?"

"Yeah, fine. Sorry, what did you say?" Her heart was racing a little.

"I'll just go to the loo..."

Daisy went through the back yard to the ladies'. She tried to remember if she had eaten anything. Her head was whirling a bit. She peered into the mirror above the basin, and sloshed cold water onto her face. "You should have eaten something, Marguerite. Had a proper meal." She wheeled round, but there was nothing to see. Just the voice: her mother's.

"Sure you're okay, Daiz?"

"Fine! Perhaps I'm a bit hungry..." Alice opened a packet of crisps and pushed it towards her. "Here. Look, why don't we get you something from Tony's on the way back?"

"Oh but..."

"Come on. I told Bryn I'd be back about now anyway."

Clutching a parcel of plaice and chips, Daisy said goodbye to Alice at the shop door. "Look, take care, okay, Daisy? We're always here if you want us..."

Alice hugged her. "Go and eat that and have a good long sleep, I would. Don't worry about opening up on the dot in the morning. You've had a long day..."

Daisy got out salt and pepper and turned on the late news. "That stuff's very bad for you. All that fat and carbohydrate."

"Mother? Mum?"

But there was no one there. Groucho snored peacefully under the kitchen table. The next morning, Daisy woke with a bit of a headache, and put her strange hallucination down to a stressful day and too much cider on an empty stomach.

The next three weeks passed without incident. Spring was advancing, and she took in a stock of new potatoes and spring onions, arranged for the peas, spoke to Graingers about tomatoes and to someone at the College about the work-experience student, and visited her mother on Wednesday afternoons as usual. These visits were not so much distressing as perplexing. What do you say to someone so completely oblivious to your presence? She chatted with the nurses about such matters as bed-sores, liquid intake and pain. The staff seemed to treat the semi-comatose Mrs Thompson with an affection that Daisy found disconcerting.

Ordinarily, her mother would never have submitted to being kissed by anyone, let alone strangers. But now Daisy dutifully kissed her mother's crêpey forehead, and said "Till next week, then, Mum," and felt a little silly. The evenings were lighter, so when the shop closed at five-thirty, she drove to Barford Common and took Groucho for a good walk where she could let him off the lead, before returning to the shop to stock shelves and chuck any item that had gone over in the compost bin.

One afternoon, she was anxious to get back in time to speak to the compost collector about another bin. She called Groucho. The air was fresh, pungent with scents of spring. New grass and budding gorse beneath a blustery sky. She saw something disappearing behind a gorse bush. A black tail? She called again. No dog. She cursed. The Common was almost eerily deserted – mostly there would be at least one other person with a dog, or a jogger; often the place was quite crowded in fine weather. "Groucho!" She began, a little, to panic, and headed for the van. Her boot struck a stone, and she stumbled.

When she looked up, her mother was standing in front of her, dressed in a dark blue coat and a headscarf.

"Mum!" cried Daisy in disbelief. But the apparition did not answer, and within a second had vanished. Daisy felt herself shiver all over. Suddenly, the dog came galloping up behind her, wagging his tail, big brown eyes contrite. After bundling him into the back of the van, she headed home at top speed. "You've forgotten your seat-belt, Marguerite," said her mother's voice. Swerving into the verge, she recovered the road just in time. There was no one in the van apart from Groucho, who had registered the swerve with a grunt but was otherwise unperturbed.

She rang Fairview. "Hullo Doreen...is my mother okay?" Asking 'Is she still in her bed, or has she died?' would have sounded as crazy as she was beginning to feel. Doreen went to check, and reported that the old dear was as right as rain, which struck Daisy as so absurd that she nearly laughed out loud. She stirred scrambled eggs, frowning. I was stone cold sober. The dog didn't turn a hair... Face it, Daisy. This is in your head, and you are going mad... She googled Alzheimer's again, hunting for heredity and symptoms that included seeing and hearing things that were not there.

Sometimes it was just her mother's voice, always calling her Marguerite (Daisy had re-named herself, and Mrs Thompson had not approved) and sometimes it was a vision – just a glimpse, or sometimes it lasted for several unnerving seconds. Mostly, Mrs Thompson appeared outside, and was always dressed differently each time: a dark coat, or her church-going frock and navy blazer, sometimes in a headscarf, sometimes with her grey hair neatly waved, and always, Daisy noted, in clothes that were familiar, clothes that, very reluctantly, Daisy had given to charities when she had sorted her mother's bungalow in order to sell it to pay for the Home.

"You think I'm crazy, don't you, Alice?" Sympathetic, sensible Alice would take her seriously and advise her. Over glasses of wine in Daisy's flat, Alice listened without interrupting. Then she said, "Daisy dear. Perhaps – I mean, I think you just have to forgive yourself. She couldn't consent to you selling her home, and you feel guilty. *She's* not haunting you, Daisy, you're haunting yourself..."

She suggested Bryn's cousin Trevor, a qualified psychotherapist in Barford. "I probably need a strait-jacket," Daisy said, biting her lip. "It's not *like* that, Daisy. He'll help you. He's very good. Um – is she here now?"

Daisy shook her head. But the moment Alice had gone, and Daisy was washing up the glasses at the sink: "I never liked that woman. All those children! Useless hippies, I say, living on the state."

"Oh, Mum, honestly. Bryn's a carpenter. And they've only got four kids." I'm arguing with her, Daisy thought. I'm actually *arguing* with her... "Go away! For God's sake, Mother, just go *away!*"

"Don't blaspheme, dear," said Mrs Thompson.

But Mrs Thompson did not 'go away'. There were, however, some Mrs Thompson-free zones, such as the shop, and, apart from that first time in the pub, whenever Daisy was in company. She became almost relentlessly sociable as a result, and spent a great deal of her free time among the broccoli and onions, installing a small TV in the little office at the back. Bryn's cousin Trevor listened, then shook his handsome grizzled head. "The psyche is the most delicate part of our anatomy," he said gravely. "And the most elusive. We treat it badly, even ignore its existence, and it comes back to bite us."

"You're saying I'm mad?" said Daisy.

"My dear woman. What, after all, is madness? The unintegrated psyche rebels until it becomes whole. It's not going to be a very rapid process, you know. Projections like these never are…"

"Oh dear," said Daisy, paying him and signing up for an initial ten sessions, blenching a little at the cost. "Well at least you've come across this sort of thing before…"

"Many times. Don't worry, Daisy. Next Thursday?" Trevor Mazey had twinkling dark eyes behind serious-looking spectacles. He twinkled at Daisy as he saw her to the door. "See Elsa at The Barford Apothecary. She'll give you something to calm things down a bit. She's probably still open now."

Elsa Dunton, who wore a professional-looking white coat, and whose shop smelled powerfully of rosemary and thyme, sent Daisy away with St.John's Wort pills and a leaflet advising dosage.

Perhaps it was the St John's Wort, or perhaps it was the feeling that, by seeing professionals, she was taking charge, Daisy began to feel a little better. Her mother's voice continued to intrude on her solitary hours, but now she answered back, cheerfully, and without undue anxiety.

"Okay, Mum. Whatever you say." I'm accepting her, she thought. She's here. It's a bore, that's all. Just a *bore…* Mrs Thompson seemed not to enjoy being 'a bore', however, and began to dress up – first as an Victorian upper servant in fustian and a bonnet and shawl, then as a pantomime witch, in a tall hat and cloak… Daisy even laughed. Perhaps it was the *menopause!* Daisy threw herself into preparations for the Summer Fayre with gusto. But then she began to feel actually physically unwell. At first, she thought it was something she had eaten. Or someone had brought a bug into the shop.

When she had not been able to face food for four days, she made an appointment with the surgery in Bagworth. "I just need something to stop the squits," she said, wanly. "And I ache all over..."

Dr Wainwright examined her, asked about her periods and looked at her notes on the computer screen. "This is your first visit for two years, Ms Thompson. Are you generally well?"

Daisy assured her that she was.

"Are you taking anything else? Any other medication?"

"No. Well, the odd aspirin... Vitamin B..." Felicity Wainwright raised an eloquent eyebrow. In this district, almost all her patients were taking 'something else'.

"Oh!" said Daisy, colouring. "I have been taking St John's Wort. I didn't think it counted."

"Why?" Dr Wainwright had piercing blue eyes and iron grey hair worn short and business-like. She reminded Daisy of a long ago science mistress at school. "Why didn't you think that St John's Wort counted?"

"Well, I mean it's just... It's a herb, isn't it? A plant?"

"So is henbane, Ms Thompson. And foxgloves. And rhubarb leaves, as I imagine you would know very well." The doctor sighed. "People will persist in the notion that just because it grows, it must either be harmless or actively good."

"Oh, but I always prefer alternative remedies if I can," said Daisy.

The doctor almost spat. "Round here, it seems to me, people can never get it through their silly heads that if it were scientifically proven to be any good, it wouldn't be 'alternative'. Or that poison plants are as 'natural' as cabbages. I take it St John's Wort means you've been feeling anxious."

"I – well – I..." And the whole story came tumbling out. Dr Wainwright proved oddly sympathetic – she had at one time treated Daisy's mother – and Daisy had come away with an appointment to see a Dr Savage at the Severn & Thames General Hospital, and strict instructions to flush the St John's Wort down the lavatory.

"A psychiatrist! What am I to *do*?" Alice cleared the remains of a vegetable pasta bake from the big family table. Lately, Daisy had been a regular supper guest. Bryn was rolling a large joint. "You smoke this, Daiz..."

Cannabis was rather good. Daisy had forgotten just quite *how* good. "And I don't even smoke!" She accepted a little bag of Bryn's home-grown. She had to be careful, however. The work-experience boy was starting next week, so she opened the windows and disguised the unmistakable aroma with joss-sticks. "Filthy things," said her mother's voice, very agitated. "Papist!"

Elliott Derry, a pleasant lad of seventeen, began work as her temporary assistant. He was doing A Levels (Economics, Business Studies) at Barford College and hoping, he told her, to go into food retail close to the production end.

"The greengrocer trade?"

"Actually, I was hoping for Marks & Sparks," he grinned. It was while showing him the stock lists on the computer – "It's far more high-tech than I expected, Daisy," – that Mrs Thompson shimmered into view, wearing a cooking overall.

"Is anything up, Daisy?"

"What? Oh, no, nothing. Nothing at all. It's a question of checking the goods in against the suppliers... Robinson's is roots... carrots, potatoes, turnips... excuse me a minute, Elliott." She dashed upstairs, breathing unsteadily.

"It's the first time it's happened in front of anyone *else*... It's getting worse, worse! I don't know what to do!" She wasn't lying on a couch, but sitting in an armchair while Dr Savage, a youngish man who urged her to call him Paul, sat opposite in another chair taking notes. "You miss her?"

"Well, hardly! How can I? When she's always here... there." To her utter dismay, Daisy burst into tears. "Silly crying won't help, Marguerite," said her mother, and Daisy gave a little scream.

"You're hearing her now?"

"Yes. Didn't you?"

"No, Daisy, I didn't. Your mother's voice is in your head, Daisy. In your imagination."

"It – it seems so real..."

"I know it does, Daisy."

"I'm mad, aren't I? Hearing voices, seeing things..."

"Tell me about your childhood, Daisy. Tell me about your mother..."

"Where are Bryn and the kids?" The big kitchen was unusually quiet. Alice was baking bread.

"Bryn's finishing a door, Jared's got football, Freya's staying with Holly, and the twins went to that Lizards gig in Bristol. Cup of tea? I'm expecting a friend any moment..." Alice wiped floury hands and poured.

"Who?"

"Juno O'Connor. A friend from Bath. I think you'll like her. She makes jewellery."

"Oh. How nice." Since Daisy had been seeing Paul Savage, she had been unusually subdued.

"She's also a healer, Daisy. Very *special*."

"Oh..."

Juno O'Connor arrived as dusk fell, an enormous woman, very tall as well as very fat, and wearing an extraordinary collection of beads and bangles that jangled. Her hair was a shade of deep plum, and she apologised for being late in a tiny voice that sounded strange coming from so large a person. "Right! I have to go and get Jared," said Alice, excusing herself. "I'll stay and chat to Jinny. Help yourselves to anything."

Daisy found it surprisingly easy to talk to Juno. "I think this psychiatrist bloke means well. Bryn's cousin Trevor, too..."

"But it hasn't helped?"

"No. I mean this – *she* – she's still there...more and more now...and I'm not getting any better."

"And why do you expect to get better, Daisy?"

"Well, I mean – I'm seeing things, aren't I? Going rapidly barmy..."

"Hold my hand." Juno O'Connor took Daisy's small square hand in her huge be-ringed one and stared into Daisy's eyes. "You know you're approaching this from the wrong way up, don't you, Daisy? No, keep looking at me." The little-girl voice was strangely compelling, the eyes a shade of inky grey.

"What – what do you mean?"

"I mean that the shrinks have been treating you as if you're ill, like this is coming from inside of you."

"But I mean it must be, mustn't it?"

"I think, Daisy, we need to assume the very opposite. Your mother is coming to *you*, seeking you out. She has something to say to you, and we must find out what it is."

"You mean – she's *real*?"

"Oh yes. Why ever not?"

"But – well, I mean – even if I believed in ghosts, whatever, she isn't dead! She can't come *back* because she hasn't *gone...*"

"Daisy, how much do we know of that hinterland between life and the thing we call death? Your mother's spirit is hovering, half in this world, half in the next, trapped in a living body and longing to flee. We have to find out what she wants, and help her. Are you prepared to do that?"

"Yes. I mean, I don't know..." Daisy suddenly felt afraid.

"Try, Daisy. Look at me, ignore everything but my eyes. Concentrate. If she will come to us now, we can question her." Daisy stared, and concentrated. But just when she was actually wanted, Mrs Thompson failed to appear. "I think she's having a little game with us," Juno said after a very long time. "Has she been here before? To Alice's house?"

"No. Not yet..."

"Then perhaps I can come to your house tomorrow," said Juno. "We need to be somewhere where her spirit is happy to be..."

When Daisy got home, her mother was sitting in an armchair, untangling some knitting, softly laughing. "It's not remotely funny. What do you want, Mum?" But Mrs Thompson just gave a last enigmatic smile, and disappeared very slowly, leaving the knitting until last. But when Juno came next day, Mrs Thompson remained obstinately absent. "Come and visit me in Bath, Daisy. I think we need to call her properly."

On Wednesday, Daisy sat regarding Mrs Thompson's face for a long time. It was strangely smooth, the shallow breaths blowing out the flaccid bluish lips like a cartoon fish. She was too weak, they said, for them to get her dressed, take her to the day room. And the TV upset her. She got agitated. Much better just to lie quietly like this. They turned her regularly, for the bed-sores, and look, now there was this special mattress to prevent the chafing. Eating? Well, not much, really, if Doreen was honest, she's using so little energy, you see. Oh, yes, Daisy. We make sure she's drinking plenty. Keep the waterworks going, and that nasty infection's gone at last. The new antibiotics have worked a treat, haven't they, darlin'? Doreen kissed Mrs Thompson's forehead.

Daisy remembered, absurdly, a long ago picnic when she had been stung by a wasp. Vinegar sloshed on her plump little thigh. She had howled, as any small child might. 'Brown Owl' had hugged her, and other mothers had been sympathetic, while other little Brownies had stared as children do. "Come along now, Marguerite. We don't let the side down, now do we?" Her mother had been brisk, plucked her up from the cooing maternal throng, given her a little shake. Five year old Daisy had stopped crying. Fifty year old Daisy could not recall her mother ever really hugging her.

Still, she had been splendid, had Daisy's mother, struggling on a widow's pension, working in Barford Library, always strong, a little embattled, essentially decent. Daisy had grown up, rebelling very little compared with most, obedient in all the essentials. "Don't throw yourself away on any Tom, Dick or Harry!" And Daisy had not. "Think for yourself, not for other people!" And Daisy had, going to College, learning about small business economics and vegetables, working for Waitrose and then starting 'Five A Day' on a bank loan. Her mother was opinionated, but had interfered very little. Why now? "You have to stop this, Mum," said Daisy softly to the tiny figure in the bed. "Leave me alone, now. Hear me, Mum? Please. Leave me alone!"

But Mrs Thompson would not leave her daughter alone. She was dressed as Margaret Thatcher when Daisy returned to the shop. "You don't know the very *first* thing about me, do you, dear?" "Go *away*!" Daisy's hand hovered over the telephone, but somehow, the thought of what Juno might *do...*

It wouldn't hurt to leave Elliott minding the shop for the afternoon. Good for him, even. She needed to walk, get away. She wandered up the High Street distractedly. Then she spotted Mrs Spears being wheeled in the opposite direction by her daughter Fran. The last people she wanted to see! Rumble's Bakery or the Cheney Newsagent? On impulse, she darted across the road and fled into the churchyard.

The Reverend Ben Newbold was an old friend. An unlikely clergyman, he wore his straggly hair in a pony tail, dressed in denims and a clerical tee-shirt. "Completely loco!" her mother had pronounced. "Daisy!" Ben was a hugging vicar, and hugged her. "I've not forgotten! Tally and I will be on parade at the meeting."

"Sorry?"

"The Fayre. Daisy, is anything up?"

"No, no, Ben. I'm fine! Busy, you know. I've got a student..." "Ah! Well done you! Great to have the young really involved, I say. Vital these days. How's poor old Mum?"

Daisy looked round, suddenly alarmed. Her mother had been right: St Michael was a splendid old building, early perpendicular, and the last place that should have been turned into a sort of Village Hall with its festoon of children's pictures and an apologetic little alter which bore nothing but a white cloth and some lilac blossom, and never used the fourteenth century pulpit because the Rev. Ben preferred to be on the same level as his neighbours, and ran services with hugs and hand-shakes, up-beat hymns sung to a guitar and prayers that almost never mentioned God. Daisy, who seldom mentioned God either except in vain, suddenly thought that He (and not 'She' and not some neutered 'It') might be offended by all this nudging familiarity, but she said suddenly, "Ben. Do you know anyone who does exorcisms?"

Ben Newbold, as vigorous a Moderniser who had ever taken the Cloth, had found a niche in Cheney Magna, where he justified his untraditional ministry to the See with bums, as he put it, on pews, recognized a neighbour in trouble when he saw one. "You're not mad, Daisy, love," he said, putting a large pastoral hand on Daisy's shoulder. "We're going to pray together, okay?"

"Okay," said Daisy.

"Dear Deity, Father Mother God, Creator of the Living Universe, who sees our hearts and knows our minds..." began the Reverend Ben, and Daisy's mother, in a hat with a veil, rolled her eyes to heaven.

"Young Ben Newbold. Great bloke." Daisy was thinking the Reverend Lawrence was cast in the same mould, until he said, heartily, "We almost never agree on anything, Ben and I. I'm an old-fashioned Good and Evil man, and I'm fond of Bach and the St James Version, and I have to beware the vanity of antiquity not to mention the venial lure of music, but Ben – well, Ben just takes care of lost souls. Good at it too. He welcomes everyone, and *I* say, what else might a Saviour approve of? Hmm? Tell me, Daisy."

She tried to explain. "She might be quite happy I'm talking to you. She was – traditional, if that's the right word. Neither High nor Low. I – I wasn't. I mean, I wasn't anything. Perhaps I shouldn't even be here…"

"But you had hope, if not faith, that the Lord might help?"

"I just thought it was worth a try…Sorry."

"Many have come to God in this manner, Daisy."

"It's only because of *her*…"

"I understand. But you know I can't exorcise a spirit still living," said the Rector of Blaston, frowning. "This is unusual, I have to say. Most unusual. I think, Daisy, that I should like to see your mother."

"But she won't come to order. I've tried. She's very obstinate…"

"I mean, Daisy, would you allow me to accompany you to your mother's sick bed?"

Daisy felt oddly comforted, as if she had found a 'cure' – not for herself, but for her mother. When Mrs Thompson wandered into the yard as she was depositing some aged cabbages, Daisy said, "It'll all be okay now, Mum. I'm going to bring the Rector to see you on

Wednesday." But on Tuesday, Daisy received a call. "Daisy? It's Doreen. I'm really sorry, but I think your Mum's going..." Daisy drove to the Home in a daze, getting stuck in traffic on the bypass. She arrived about ten minutes too late. Her mother's tiny body was propped up on pillows. She looked entirely peaceful. Dr Mahmood met her. "It was more sudden than we expected, Daisy. I'm very sorry there wasn't more warning for you. She was very frail these past days..."

Daisy lay in bed. She could hear Elliott Derry's mother downstairs in the shop. She ought to be grateful that Sue Derry had come to the rescue. Everything was in good hands. The Derrys were feeding Groucho, taking him for walks... The Fayre had come and gone. Alice said it didn't matter – they had missed her, but they'd coped. Alice brought home-made soup and her own bread. Shortly she would get up, get back to everything properly... but something heavy and unshiftable seemed to have descended on her chest, on her limbs, and she couldn't be bothered to move. A half-completed crossword lay at her side. She had paused *Pride & Prejudice* in the middle of episode one, and the screen whirled green, red, orange.

"Daisy? It's Alice." Alice's deep brown eyes were full of consternation. "Let me know what I can do, love... I'm here. Have you had your soup?"

"A bit."

"Daisy..."

"I'll be fine, Alice. Fine. You're so kind."

"Has she...?"

"No. Nothing. Not since..." And then Daisy began, softly at first, to weep.

Samuel Esau studied at De Montfort University and at the London Metropolitan University, where he graduated in BA English Literature and Creative Writing.

Samuel Esau has always enjoyed writing stories, and can claim to be a prolific author, with many works from over the years. Birthright was his final piece from the final year of his course, and the writing of the larger novel of which this piece of work will eventually become a part is already well under way.

Birthright

'A single drop can sprout the seed of doubt into a towering tree.'

A single drop of water. What happened that night- or rather, early morning- counted as more than just one drop in my book. At least a trickle of water, like getting squirted in the face by some tacky 99p water pistol, the kind you could get from a stall at any car-boot sale… But the analogy still worked. Before then; sure, half of the questions had always been there, but they'd never been solid, always shifting, growing or shrinking with the times. It wasn't fair, but that was just the way the world worked. But when that drop of water splashed across my face, the revelation that there was something where the cosy, mundane world explanation just didn't work, couldn't work; that was all they would need to take root…

On the headcount, there had to be, what, fifty? Sixty? Definitely more than forty people. Teens, juveniles, and a fair few guys in their twenties baying for virgin girls- and that was just out in the back garden. This was supposed to have been my party, celebrating my A-level results, but even if all five of my invitees had come, it still wouldn't have been more than a speck in the background of little sister's shindig. Right now, there were probably more people cramped in the downstairs bathroom than there had been on my entire guest list. As for trumping me on the decibel count, well, that had been a dead cert from the start. I liked my music, yeah, but I liked my hearing too, and I planned on keeping it into old age. Even out here, I could already feel the abuse taking its toll on my ear-bones, pounding my eardrums into numbness.

What was I doing here? I knew where Marshall had gone, off to spend the rest of his night out on the town. I could blow this place, join him out on his booze cruise, and Mum and Dad would never have a clue. Lili wouldn't give a fuck what I did even if she was stone-cold sober, and she's been draining those bottles and puffing those spliffs for hours now. I mean, come on, what's stopping me...? CRASH. Loud enough to hear through it all, the sound of shattering porcelain coming from the kitchen, the third to get smashed in just a few minutes, answered the question for me. If I left the place to Lili's devices, chances are there wouldn't be a liveable home to come back to. Where the hell was she?

But I already knew the answer. She'd be standing over in the corner of the living room, just inside the wide-open patio door, inches away from one of the blaring, shoulder-height speakers, lapping up as much of the limelight as she could, as usual. Not that I'd be able to see her. The crowd of schoolgirls clustered up in that corner were all on Lili's 'A-list', made up of some of the wildest party animals, glossiest gossips and bitchiest bitches in Barnet, and they'd been following her around everywhere since we opened the doors, penning her in for the last four hours straight. Even if I somehow managed to break through, went up in her face and yelled at the top of my voice, Lili wouldn't be able to hear me- if she actually wanted to listen to anything I had to say. *Fat chance...*

And that wasn't even the worst of it, not by a long way. I'd lived here more than half of my life, so I knew the layout of this place with my eyes closed- and I needed every scrap of spatial memory I could call upon. Stepping through the back door into the house, everything beyond the reach of my fingertips was just a pale grey blur in the whiteout- another few steps further in, and I couldn't even make out my forearms any more. With the visibility levels in here, you'd have thought that a riot squad had launched a volley of smoke canisters in through the windows- but to find out what it really was, all you had to do was take a whiff of the stuff and it all became clear. *I put a freaking poster up on the front door laying out the law, I even told half of the bastards to their face on the way in for fuck's sake, and still these addicts can't get it through their thick heads that no, means no, MEANS NO...!*

I took a moment's pause, pulling my shirt collar up over my mouth as a makeshift filter before pushing on forward until I could feel the wall with my outstretched hands, then feeling my way around to the other side of the wall, through the living room- where the smoke was thicker than anywhere else, but the visible impact of the smoke rings generated by the speakers' blast waves meant you could still see practically everything in there- and out into the hall, glancing towards the glut of stoned school kids either leant back against the walls or sprawled out on the floor as I picked a path through them all.

This was my home, our home, and even though Lili's guests and gatecrashers were the ones trashing everything in sight, I knew full well who'd be taking the blame when Mom and Dad got back. But what could I do? Even a professional bouncer crew would probably have given up by this stage. To try and bring this raving rabble back under some semblance of control now, on my own, without anything to back it up. What with the illicit drugs, fags and alcohol- for the ninety percent or so who were still kids, none of it was legal- I didn't even want to think what kind of heat they'd be packing. Blades of all shapes and sizes; flick-knives, knuckledusters, machetes- and you knew there had to be at least one concealed firearm in there... I didn't have a death wish. The situation down here was a lost cause. But maybe, just maybe, there might still be something left to save...

Upstairs. Those child safety gates, at the top and the bottom of the stairs, were installed just after we moved in eleven years ago, when little Lili was already five years old, and there had never been any reason for having them there when she could just vault over them- the same option I took now, a lot less hassle than fumbling around in my pockets for the key- but the gates had always been strong enough, and right now, they were nothing short of a godsend. Proper barriers to blockade the only way upstairs, to keep the flood welling up from the depths at bay- and walking up to the foot of the stairs, you could see that somehow, miraculously, the lower gate was still closed, with the latch still locked up tight. And if no-one's used the gate, then upstairs should have been clear, untouched by the minions of chaos down below. Unless they did the same thing as I just did...

The noise from those boom-boxes ebbed away as I walked up the stairs, the air getting a lot clearer as well, enough for me to run the risk of taking my collar off my face and breathing it in. Glancing back down at the scene in the hallway, covered in that dense blanket of second-hand smog; it was like looking down on a storm cloud from an airliner soaring high up above it all. But the momentary lapse back into optimism didn't last long. Jumping over had been easy enough. The risk of that lot out in the hallway thinking I was inviting them to come on up, and storming the gateway soon as I'd taken the lock off, had been averted. The upper gate, though- yawning wide open, despite the fact I'd closed it earlier, putting the latch on even if I hadn't been able to find anything to lock it up with- made it blatant enough that I hadn't been the first to go over the top tonight.

So much for R&R. I'll have to clear out whoever's already up here, and whatever handiwork they'll have left behind, room by room. *I swear, if my room isn't pristine, if I find one thing out of place, I'm going into Lili's and cutting all the clothes in her wardrobe up into doilies...* First things first, though. Checking up on the state of my bedroom would have to wait. There were still gatecrashers up here. From the noise they were making, it wasn't rocket science working out which room they were in, or what it was they were getting up to in there. I walked across the landing to the door opposite, and pulled it open. Dad's study was the smallest room in the house, and the only room without a window, so you could understand if they wanted the privacy; but still, looking at the scene in here, you had to wonder why they didn't go in one of the rooms with an actual bed.

The guy was standing in front of the reclining leather armchair in the middle of the room, with his back to the door, his pants down around his ankles, and his girl lying prone in the armchair with only her legs visible on either side, knees on the armrests, spread-eagled wide enough to rustle Dad's stacked paperwork on the desk with her left foot and brush the wall with her right. The two of them were too engrossed in the task at hand to even notice the door had been opened, rocking the reclining armchair back and forth, with their panting, grunting and moaning almost overwhelmed by its squeaking protest. If this had been somewhere other than my house, or even a few hours earlier, I'd practically be rolling around on the floor laughing, but I wasn't in the mood for fun and games. Well, let's get this over with...

"*Ah-hem.*" No response. If anything, now the guy was thrusting his hips even harder, faster, trying to build towards his climax. *Oh no you don't...*

"Oi! The two of you, out! Now!"

This time, I got a response. The girl shrieked at the top of her voice, flailing her legs in her frantic efforts to escape the confines of the armchair as fast as she could. On the desk, only one or two folders got left behind, with the rest of them sent flying, Dad's meticulously catalogued paperwork scattered across the room like so many worthless election leaflets. Still intent on working away, trying to keep her in the chair and keep himself inside her, the guy leaned in to whisper something, attempting to calm her down. He failed. Still squealing incoherently at the highest volume and pitch she could achieve, the girl managed to break the link, leaping out of the armchair, snatching up her pile of clothes from the floor and managing to get them all back on in barely ten seconds.

"Ahh, *come on.* Come on! Nah, *don't..."*

But lover-boy's pleas were ignored, Little Miss Bashful brushing me to the side to rush out of the room, across the landing and back down the stairs. Pulling his jeans back up to sit just below his hips, the guy scowled as he watched her leave. Eyes narrowed, teeth bared, sweat trickling down his brow from his unrewarded exertions, he tossed a brief, intense glare my way before chasing out after her, leaving me still standing there just inside the doorway, alone in the study with the damage. I took a half step backwards, slumping back against the doorway as the scene they had left behind started to sink in. "Where the heck do I begin?"

There was a small trickle of some kind of clear fluid, which had to be either sweat or something even worse, running slowly down the seat of the armchair. On the floor, I could see where the guy's stretched, discarded protection had fallen, with the tip jutting out from underneath the desk- no way I was picking that up with my bare hands- and the jumbled, newly creased sheets of paper were everywhere, strewn across every surface in the room. I kicked four or five pieces of paper off their resting place on top of my feet, scattering them across the floor with the rest, before walking back in and closing the door behind me- somehow managing to get two sheets wedged between the door and the frame in the process... "*Oh, fuck.* Like this shit wasn't hard enough already."

I managed to jump in and stop it closing completely, but one of them- *last month's account sheet for the Chinatown supermarket, brilliant-* had already been crumpled up like an accordion. The other one wasn't even damaged though- kind of. It hadn't quite been laminated, but the A4 sheets of clear plastic on either side, tied in place with string threaded through holes in each corner, had still managed to do protect it well enough. It hadn't been creased or bent in the slightest, but the paper in the middle looked tatty, aged. Some of the words, written on it in Mandarin, were so faded you could hardly- *read them...*

I did a double take, stared at the words scrawled across the middle of the sheet, with *my name* right in the centre of it all, together with my date of birth just under eighteen years ago. A birth certificate. *It had to be-* but what was it that Mum and Dad said, when I tried to get my driver's licence? When we opened my student loan account? '*You don't have a birth certificate! You never did, the PRC hospital never gave us one.*' Why would they keep this from me? Unless there was something, *in this sheet,* that they felt they had to hide. Vaguely aware of the sheets of paper I was blindly trampling through to get there, I walked across to the desk, pulling myself up on top of the desktop to take the weight off my legs, *with every answer I could come up with mushrooming into a dozen more questions...*

Why didn't it say anything about the time of day, or the place of birth? And written right at the bottom of the sheet, blown up largest of all, was the number- No, wait; *cost? 5,000 Yuan?* That's just *crazy*... But that was nothing compared to the detail in the small print. How the fuck could I possibly have been *six weeks old*, on the day I was...? No. The day, I was *supposed to have been* born. The photocopier was sitting in the corner, opposite the door, and I glided across to it as if in a dream, turned it on, and started taking the sheet of limp card out from between the two slides of plastic...

*

'All Deceit dies in the end, but Truth lives eternal.'

By the time I went to bed that morning, with the sun well above the horizon, trying to get some rest- and amazingly enough, almost managing it- the handful of scattered seeds had sprung up like a bamboo forest, growing until it towered above everything, overshadowing all else. A lie- No, LIES, who knew how many lies- had been told, I knew that now... I would get to the bottom of this. I wasn't going to confront them with it like an idiot, but somehow, eventually, in the course of the next week, I would manage to coerce it out of them. At least, that was my original plan. Of course, when Mum and Dad actually got back, things ended up panning out very differently...

"I still can't believe it. All of this. I trusted you, Zhāng Wu, to keep the house in order for one night. *One night...*"

I said nothing, sitting down at the kitchen table and pouring out my cereal into one of the few bowls which had escaped with chips out of their rim, instead of being shattered into fragments. Opposite, Dad was polishing off the last remnants of his omelette, toast and plum tomatoes. Lounging back in his seat, his bare feet up on the table on either side of his plate, shaking his head and throwing those accusing stares in unison with everything Mum said.

"...then we come back to find this, this *carnage*? Wu, I am so disappointed in you!"

I could have had a go, tried to drum it into their heads that IT WASN'T MY FAULT, there was nothing I could have done to stop things getting out of hand; but I was too tired, too fed up with it all to bother with a response. A response which, based on the fact that I'd already tried on each of the- *six? Or was it seven now? So hard to keep track-* of the accusations I'd been peppered with since they woke me up this morning, around half an hour ago, wouldn't do me any good anyway.

Needless to say, little Lili had been left in peace to get her beauty sleep, even after I told them who had trashed the place. She'd brought them here, she'd encouraged them to go wild, drink, snort, inject as they pleased, but still, even after all that, what did I hear? '*You are the oldest. You are not just a boy any more, you are nearly 18! You are a man! We left you in charge of the house, not her, and YOU let us down! No, we don't want to hear it. You always make your excuses, but you can never, ever, shoulder your responsibilities like a real man!* I swear, I'm just, "*So tired,* of all this BULL-shit."

"*What* did you just say?" Oh. I just said that out loud, didn't I? *Brilliant...* Groaning, I finished the job of pouring the milk- whole, not semi-skimmed- on top of the Cookie Crisp cereal, pretending to be engrossed in the task of pushing the pieces floating on top below the surface with my spoon. I didn't have to look up to sense Dad's fierce glare singeing through my fringe like a laser, trying to get the burning beam into my eyes. Over to the left, I could hear Mum turning off the tap in the kitchen sink, the sound of whatever vegetables she'd been washing being plopped back down on the work surface. I knew full well what was coming next. *You've felt the quakes, now here comes the tsunami...*

"Sometimes, Wu, you make me question whether you are really our son."

What? What kind of...? Thrown off balance, not just by the words but the perfectly level, sincere tone, I sat back up straight in the chair, turning around to face- the back of Mum's head, with the tap already turned back on, the task of rinsing the spring onions already resumed. Like I wasn't even worth talking to directly- like it wasn't even an insult, or a confrontation, but just stating the facts. Incensed, my chest puffing upwards and outwards of its own accord, I turned back around to face Dad, watched him lean back in his chair, shaking his head from side to side in the most maddening, condescending manner possible, over and over again, his smirking gaze still never leaving my own. The scene seemed to melt into itself as the boiling frustration encroached inwards like a heat-haze; but the image of that tattered 18 year old sheet of paper kept imposing itself above all else, until the real world was nothing more than fuzzy scenery in the background.

"You took the words right out of my mouth..."

Now, I got a response. In an instant, Mum had shifted from her nonchalant pose to stand bolt upright. The splashing noises stopped, with the water from the tap allowed to flow freely again. A second later, the half-rinsed onions dropped into the sink with a thud. Dad froze in mid-motion, with his head halfway over to the left. The room fell deadly silent; my retort left hanging in the air like the threat of a loaded gun... Three seconds. Four... Mum slumped forward over the sink, shuddering, with visible spasms running across her back. It took another moment or two before the realisation hit home, that she was actually properly crying over it. Dad's face contorted into that of a raving psychopath, his eyes bulging out of their sockets, eyebrows pulled downwards, with his nostrils, already freakishly large for a Han Chinaman, puffing further and further outwards- and still, time ticked on. Nine seconds. Ten. Then...

"What did you...?"

"You know full well what I just said! I know you heard me, loud and clear-" BANG. Dad slammed his fist down with all the force he could manage, leaping up out of his seat and leaning forward across the table, putting on a convincing impression of a posturing gorilla. The table shuddered; my spoon slid off its perch on the rim of the breakfast bowl, a few drops of milk splashing up as it dived for cover below the surface.

"WU! You *will* take that back. Take that back! Apologise, to me and your mother, right this second! *How could you* say such a hurtful thing?"

I pushed myself to my feet, hard, taking out a few moments' worth of frustration by toppling the chair over onto its back, sending it skidding along the kitchen tiles and crashing back into the fridge-freezer.

"How could *I...*? You asked the question, not me! You're the one who brought it up; you're the one who disowns me every time anything happens to me, or around me. No matter who does it, it *always* has to fall on *my shoulders. My fault alone, my burden to bear...* Proper parents would at least *try* to understand, they would be there for me, support me- but not you! *Oh no, not you.* You never have, and you never will. No *real* parent would treat me the way you do, the way either of you two do."

"How DARE YOU! That's IT- Get out of our sight! Stop eating OUR food, right this second, and go up to your room! You are

GROUNDED!"

"You know what? I've got an even better idea." I turned away from my untouched breakfast on the dining table, away from both of them, and started walking. It took three steps, or stomps, to reach the door.

"*You-* Get back here! Where the hell do you think you are you going...?"

I stopped with one hand on the door handle, swung back around to face down the two of them. Across on the other side of the room, the tap was still running, with Mum still slumped over the sink, but she'd turned her head, straining her neck to look back at me over her shoulder. Just looking at her face, with the first tears already trickling down her cheeks, and more drops joining the procession every time she blinked... Her lips moved, either whispering too softly to hear over the running water, or mouthing it under her breath, but I could still make out the words. '*Please. Son...*' My grip on the handle loosened; my thumb started to fall away...

Then Dad walked across to shove himself up in my face, imposing himself in front of everything else yet again. Arms clenched across his chest, glaring down at the top of my head, still putting on his 'show of dominance'. *I have so had enough of this shit.*

"WU! Answer me, NOW!"

"I'm getting as far out of your sight as I can, out of this fucking house. Oh, and Dad, I know about that certificate, the one you've been hiding from me, *these last eighteen years.* I've seen it, read it, and I promise you, I will find out the truth. *It's only a matter of time.*"

Without looking back, I turned the handle and barged out

through the kitchen door, through the living room into the hall. Took my trainers out from the shoe rack in the cupboard under the stairs, sat down and tied up the laces, waiting all the while for Dad to come marching out after me, tossing whatever insults, or curses, or derogatory comments he could muster after me- but he never came. Except for the jingling of my keys, and the tap still running back in the kitchen sink, the silence was still unbroken, any response still unuttered when I walked out the door, and left the house behind...

*

'Will you believe in the beautiful lie? Or can you accept the terrible truth?'

I had had enough. Over an hour later, far across London on the other side of the Thames, sitting there on that bench in Kennington Park, I resolved that I would do whatever it took- that I wouldn't rest, wouldn't ease the pressure until I had prised the secret of the last eighteen years from their lips, that very day. I had no idea of just how quick and easy getting the truth would be, or just how hard it would be to take... As I re-entered the London Underground station, got back on the Northern line and began the long journey back to Barnet, I thought I had steeled myself, prepared myself for anything; but when it came, that revelation would turn my world on its head, shaking my perception of my entire existence to its foundations...

I got out the keys and unlocked the door, pushed it open and walked back through. Drenched with sweat, every inch of my skin saturated in the stuff, I pulled- *no, peeled-* off my windbreaker; casting it off onto the banister. *Man, what was I thinking anyway, taking a coat?* It's, what, over thirty degrees out there, and humid as hell! First thing I need to do is go upstairs, have a shower, and get changed into something else, 'cause these clothes probably reek of B.O. right now...

"Wu."

Leaving the untying of my shoelaces as a work-in-progress, I took my hands away, pushed myself back off the ground to stand upright, and found myself face to face with Mum. Standing straight in front of me in the hallway, so close I could have reached out and wiped the drip-drip of tears away from her chin. "Oh- hi, Mum."

"Come, into the living room."

"Yeah, just, wait a sec; let me take my shoes off."

"Wu. Son..." Dad stepped out from the living room, coming forward to stand just behind Mum, putting his left hand on her shoulder, stroking her hair with his right, nestling his chin on the top of her head. Looking at the soft undertones in his voice, the tired, relaxed posture- those same two damp patches, trailing down either side of his face- all of my frustration from earlier, which had flared up again when I'd seen his car still parked up in the driveway, flickered and died. He had been crying, anyone could see that- but Dad never cried. *Never...*

"...Come on in. We need to talk." Dad turned, walked back into the living room and pulled Mum back through the door with him, beckoning for me to follow with his trailing hand. For a moment I just stood there. Looked down at my dirty trainers, at the untied shoelaces trailing along the floor, before leaving it as it was, reaching out to stop the door from swinging shut before walking through after them. "Yes. *We do.*"

Both of them had already sat down on the sofa. Leaning

against the armrests on either side, they reached across to pat the space they'd saved for me in the middle- but if they thought I would be drawn in, placated that easily after what had happened earlier, they had another thing coming. I made a beeline straight for the armchair, falling back into it.

"Earlier, when you ran off, where did you go?"

"I dropped in at the hospital on the way back, booked some tests." Of course, it was a complete lie, one I'd ironed out when I was fumbling for the keys out on the porch- but I managed to make sure I kept my face firm, didn't blink, didn't do anything that would give the game away. "When they come back, I'm going to find out what the truth is, whether you tell me or not."

"I knew that this day would come. I always knew. We were never going keep this from him forever; he was always going to find out."

"Please, Zhuàng, I can't... Tell him..."

"Tell me- what? Well? I'm waiting." Trying to put some emphasis on it, to make the tone of my voice as cold and harsh as I could, I turned the chair around to face the sofa instead of the T.V, towards Mum and Dad. They had already shuffled across to fill the gap between them, huddled up together in the middle of the sofa now, but still shifting uncomfortably from side to side, back and forth. At last, Dad leaned forward to clasp his knees, staring down at the coffee table. When he opened his mouth to speak, the weariness in his voice was even more palpable than it was in his tired posture.

"You know, the family legacy rests on your shoulders. Our eldest son, our only son- me and your mother, would both give up our lives for yours in an instant- but biologically, genetically, you are not- we are not..."

"What are you trying to say?"

"Your mother did not give birth to you. Neither she nor I played a part in conceiving you…"

The words, what he'd just said, coursed through my head like an electric shock. Overwhelmed, my brain seemed to seize up, every thought I'd had stored up jolted out of existence in an instant. Even as the voltage started to ease off, as some traces of self-awareness began to return, it still felt like any mental activity had just flat-lined. I blinked slowly, once, twice. Slumped back in the armchair, turned my gaze away from them and towards the miniature stalactites of dried paint, up on the ceiling. It was only when the image started to get blurred, when little patches of light started to dance in front of my vision like static on a T.V screen, that I realised I wasn't actually breathing any more, put in the conscious effort needed to get my diaphragm pumping again, in, out, *in, out*… But over on the sofa, Dad was still talking. I had to fight to get it back together, to get my brain rebooted so I could listen to the rest of what he had to say.

"…Back then, back in Guizhou, we had been trying for a baby since the day we consummated our marriage. Years went by, more than a decade… all to no avail. When we finally got desperate enough to see a doctor about it, he confirmed our worst fears. I was all but barren; it would take nothing short of a miracle to ever have the child we yearned for, naturally…"

"So, that receipt, or certificate- then you had me through I.V.F?"

"No, that was your sister. The whole reason we came here in the first place, to the U.K, was so that we could escape the one child policy and have another, one who would be ours in every sense of the word- we'd already booked the treatment at the fertility clinic before even getting on the plane."

I let my head sink, setting my chin against my chest, staring down blankly at my clasped hands, resting on my stomach. Detached from it all, almost as an outside observer, I looked on as they let go of each other, fell away to either side of my body, and curled up into fists, clenching ever tighter.

"Whoa, hold up. Yours, '*in every sense of the word*'. So what the hell was I then? Why didn't I, why don't I make the grade then?"

"Your father didn't mean... You do, you are..."

Slowly, deliberately, I pushed myself up out of the armchair and walked across the room to stand in front of the sofa, bending down over the coffee table to stare them down at point-blank range. "WHY? Tell me, NOW!"

"We adopted you. Your '*mother*', the woman who gave birth to you, was more than willing to give you up from when you were barely a month old, the money mattered more to her than you ever would have; but for us, you were our chance to have the son we had always wished for, the continuation of the family line. For us, you were worth more than any sum of mere wealth..."

BANG. I lashed out at the table, slamming my fist down a few inches in front of his face, cutting him off in mid-sentence. "*Willing? The money mattered more?* How could you possibly know that, unless..." Then I stood bolt upright as it hit home, taking a couple of steps back from the coffee table, backing away from them. When I resumed talking, the frosty tone of voice wasn't just put on for dramatic effect. The same ice was spreading through my veins, pushing up goose-pimples across every inch of my body. "So then, how much did it take to convince her to give me up? To get your firstborn son, the heir that you both wanted oh so badly- *but why ask a question when you already know the answer? I've seen the receipt; I know exactly how much you bought me for…"*

Eyes half-closed, shaking my head, I turned around and started walking back the way I had come. Making my way back through the hall, I could hear Mum's frantic pleas to *let them explain, that I had to give her a chance to explain*; but now I knew the truth. I already had all the explanation I needed… The clamour of both of them getting to their feet, desperately trying to come and cut me off from wherever it was they thought I was going, probably fearing for their chances of ever seeing me again.

But I wasn't going anywhere. Instead of walking on through the front door, I put one hand on the banister at the foot of the stairs, turned through 180 degrees and started climbing. Five steps up, I brushed past Lili, still in her nightclothes, bleary-eyed from all the substance abuse last night; ignored her slurred question about what shit had been going down downstairs, and got an earful for it, a catalogue of insults and swear words that carried on until the parents rushed out into the hall down below, when I was four steps from the top. With the two of them shouting to keep me in earshot, they shoved her aside to charge up after me, closing the gap. Even Lili had to have got the gist of it by the time I reached the landing, walking across to my bedroom at the far end. I only just managed to get the door closed and locked before they barged into it, jostling to try and get it open, desperately pleading with me to *let them in*, to *try and understand…*

Gradually, I became aware of a strange, burbling noise, before realising it was actually coming from my own throat, that my eyes were watering. Was I crying, or laughing? More than five minutes later, when they finally stopped fighting with my door handle and left me alone, I still couldn't work out which…

*

'A relationship founded on a lie is diseased, only growing uglier, more twisted. Burn it down, that healthy shoots may grow from the ashes.'

The half of that day that still remained, continuing deep into the night that followed, locked up in my room trying to come to terms with what I now knew, had to be the longest of my life. The lie had been exposed; the outer layers had been peeled away, the' family' I had grown up as part of revealed as the gnarled, hollow carcass it had always been. Exposing all of those wriggling, niggling questions that had surfaced over the years, feasting on its rotting innards along with a whole host of others I had always known about, but never thought of asking. Now, I knew where the infestation came from- but my own roots lay elsewhere, not here. Not with them… The emotional gash that had been ripped open was bleeding, and it would keep dripping until I knew my whole story, from beginning to end, filling in that missing first chapter of my life. In the morning hours, with the black skies outside starting to turn grey again, I started up my P.C, went on the internet, and set about doing what had to be done. By Monday, just over a week later, the preparations had been made. It was time to go find it…

"Son? Wu? Do you want any help with that…?"

Dad- no, *Zhuàng*, put his hand on my left shoulder. I shrugged it off, picking up the pace to a brisk trot, trying to get some distance between us. Not that that would be even remotely possible when it was a constant struggle to get this trolley to go in a straight line. The thing seemed to have a suicidal mind of its own, and bearing a load that in all likelihood weighed more than I did, it was nigh-on impossible to control. It didn't matter, not enough to enlist any more of his 'help'. On the way here, since we left the house something like *four hours ago* now, I'd been window-gazing pretty much non-stop for the whole journey. Not because there'd been anything interesting out there to look at; it was all so boring, so lethargic, that I'd been fighting to keep my eyelids at bay all the way.

But if I hadn't, we'd never have got here at all. If I'd told them the real time I needed to be here for, instead of making out that I needed to be here earlier than I did, scamming them that the departure was an hour earlier than it actually was back when I was trying to get out of the house, we'd never have made it here fast enough. As it was, Zhuàng's attempts to take us off course under cover of feigned ignorance all those times along the way, sedately cruising along at more than ten mph under the speed limit for the whole journey, *fifteen* below on the motorway, meant I had barely fifteen minutes to spare by the time we got here, and what with the ten minutes it had taken to park the car, making out that his Audi 'wasn't lined up properly' again and again, crawling in and out of the space one inch at a time, stretched out each of those *eight* failed attempts for as long as possible... I didn't have time to spare for any more 'accidentally-on-purpose' delays.

I kept walking, heaving the trolley up the short ramp at the end, off the tarmac and onto the narrow pedestrianised section at the end. The arrows painted across the concrete paving marked out the right path, and I followed it onto the elevated walkway, with the flickering, incandescent yellow glow of the multi-story car park replaced by whatever pale semblance of daylight managed to filter its way through the ominous, dark-gray clouds overhead. Taking a glance upwards, I watched as a large passenger jet burst through the thick canopy, swooping in low enough on the approach to pick out the tread in the individual tires of its landing gear.

Almost nine days had passed since that fateful day when the

curtain of ignorance had come crashing down. When I finally broke my isolation in the bedroom, with the sun already high in the sky on the following day, I wasn't asking questions, or willing to answer any. I knew what had to be done; my resolve had been cast in steel, the wheels already set in motion. But it hadn't stopped them trying to toss their spanners in at every turn. On the outskirts of my field of vision, I could see Zhuàng moving in again, reaching out towards the handle of the trolley this time. I tried to keep my voice level, but I just couldn't stop that smidgen of sarcasm creeping into the first word.

"Dad, leave it. Really, I can push the trolley on my own..."

The hand kept drifting, brushing against the handlebar, but using that honorific of old had done the job. Zhuàng backed off out of arm's reach, leaving me room to breathe as we left the skybridge behind, entered the waiting lift, and pressed the button to close the doors. But it wasn't just him I had to deal with. He had been in the driver's seat on the journey here, creating every hindrance possible to try and stop me getting here; but with the doors clanging shut, and the lift slowly making its way down to the ground floor, he had already done all he could. Now, it was *her* turn to try and talk me around, to mount that desperate last attempt to turn me from the path I had chosen.

"Wu, you don't have to do this..."

If I had a pound for every time I'd heard that from Xiǎofo- '*Mum*'- in the last week, I'd have got the money spent on my ticket back with interest by now. Standing right alongside, she leaned across the trolley, staring up into my eyes, trying to make me see the show of emotion playing across her face. I looked away, casting my gaze across the minefield of freshly chewed gum wads strewn across the floor of the lift, making a mental note to avoid stepping in any of them on the way out. However, when the doors slid open, and I pushed my luggage trolley out into the congested commotion of Terminal 3, I had something more important to look out for. Looking at the layout of the place, it wasn't far, just one zone away, but it had taken long enough to get here, and I wasn't going to waste what little time I had left.

I started jogging, getting enough momentum behind the trolley to make it stop lurching around, and leaving the two of them trailing in my wake into the bargain. Hurtling through into zone F, with the KLM check-in desk coming into view, it was to find there was no queue at all, just one woman in the process of walking away... While there were still people behind the counter, the check-in should still be open. Still, it didn't stop the butterflies taking flight in my stomach as I pulled the ticket out of my pocket and charged up to the desk at full tilt, leaving the luggage trolley to crash into the unmanned Royal Amsterdam desk next door.

"Hi? Yeah, I'm here to check-in for the 16:00 flight to Guiyang."

The white guy behind the desk, a youth with his face pock-marked with acne, craned his neck to see the ticket, raising his eyebrows. "Oh, alright. KWE100? The last check-ins call went out almost ten minutes ago; but you're lucky, we haven't loaded the last few items onto the baggage cart yet. Come on, quickly."

The KLM employee waved me across to the weighing area. With cramp flaring in my legs, panting both from the mad dash and in sheer relief, I turned back to the trolley, pulling it over to the right check-in desk. Starting with the lightest item first, I picked my briefcase up off the trolley and put onto the scales.

"O.K, 4.8 kilos. Is that your hand luggage? Good, it's within the limit." Bringing it back and putting it down at my feet, I started to unclick all the straps holding my rucksack in place, slinging it off my back into the weighing area.. But now the others had caught up. Gasping to regain her breath, Xiǎofo made her way over to stand next to me, before continuing where she had left off.

"You don't have to do this, you do know that?"

Rolling my eyes in frustration, I turned back to the trolley, set about the task of getting the main suitcase out of there. "Yes, I do. You might have a hard time trying to understand, but this is something I have to do."

"But throwing away your future in exchange for your past? Giving up your studies, surrendering the place at university we fought so hard for..."

At last, I managed to pull the suitcase out over the edge. Cut off in mid-sentence, she scrambled to get out of the way as the trolley, freed of its burden, careered off in her direction. Dragging the suitcase across to the desk, I heaved it up into the weighing area, narrowly managing to stop it toppling over on top of the rucksack- not that it really mattered, given the scant care they'd take in loading it onto the plane...

"Is that everything? Alright, that's 59.1 kilos; you don't have to pay extra baggage fees."

I nodded, some semblance of a smile ghosting across my features- then evaporating in an instant as I turned back around to find myself staring into Xiǎofo's watery eyes at point blank range, yet again. "How many times do we have to go through this, over and over again, it's a GAP YEAR. Queen Mary said they'd save the place for me, I'll still be starting my BA in Journalism this time next year, what's the problem?"

Zhuàng was standing a couple of paces away, leaning against the adjoining Royal Amsterdam desk. At least he hadn't come over to shove himself in my face. Just like Xiǎofo though, he still hadn't given up on trying to talk me around. "Even now, you can turn back, come back with us…"

"No, I can't. Do you know who my real parents are? Who conceived me, gave birth to me before you purchased me? Because unless you can tell me that, I have to do this. I have to know."

"Seriously, Wu, you're like fucking obsessed…"

Lili. On the car journey, she'd been too busy chatting away on her iPhone to engage with what was going on. When the signal died on the way through the car park, and in the lift, she'd just taken out the headphones and immersed herself in her iTunes instead; but as she emerged through the crowd of people, still sauntering along at the same easy pace, you could see she'd taken them out of her ears, a broad smirk spread across her face.

"You should listen to yourself. *I must goa backa to China, to restoh my hoh-nor anda find my birthright…*"

Dropping the clichéd 'any-East-Asian' voice, Lili grinned broadly, getting her kicks from winding me up, the same as always. Glaring at her, every single detail of my life as Zhāng Wu replayed in my mind. Every last issue- all of the chores and responsibilities, the way Lili had always been their favourite by a country mile, never punished, never chastised; while I, *their first-born son…* I'd kept my increasing acrimony under lock and key all these years, but there was no reason to keep it bottled up any more.

"Yeah? Well, what do you know, bitch? I've seen you writing your name, you don't even put your surname first. Forget pronouncing your own name, you can't even spell it."

"What did you just call me?"

"Oh, what, bitch? Pampered little poodle bitch? Right, because that's all you heard, the only bit you cared about. Ickle-pickle fickle Lily Zhang, wannabe white slapper..."

"*You...* Bastard! Fucking piece of shit...!"

With Lili screeching out every expletive in her vocabulary at the top of her voice, filling the air with filth in more ways than one- I followed the trajectory of the globs of brownish spittle flying from her mouth, flecking across anything close enough- practically every bystander in zone F was staring at her now. A fair few of them were verging on hysterical laughter, the KLM guy among them. For the first time in the past week, a proper, genuine smile asserted itself on my face.

"I may not know who my real parents are, not yet- but I certainly know more about my identity than you do about yours." Reaching down to picking the briefcase back up, I started to walk through the no-go area that had materialised around her, towards the base of the nearest escalator.

"...Go on, go fuck your prostitute momma! Hope you never come back, you f..."

"*Enough!*"

Thwack. Lili reeled backwards, her eyes bulging as wide as those fake eyelashes would allow. Not from the force behind the blow, she hit her own cheeks harder than that when she was applying powder; but from the sheer psychological impact, enough to stun even her into total silence, and halt me in my tracks. *Impossible...* but Xiǎofo was still standing over her, her open hand still raised and ready. I'd imagined it so many times, but never dreamed I would ever see it, *Lili getting disciplined...*

"Wu, please, your sister..." Zhuàng walked across to cut off my path, imploring me to come to the same reasoning they had. To wave it all away, say that it didn't matter, that things could be reconciled with a click of our fingers... But I knew the truth now. However much they'd tried to hide it, claiming every disparity as some warped, feeble attempt at equal treatment, I always knew I had never been anything more to my parents than a second-class child. It would take more than one action, one wet-wipe to mop the dirt off that slate. I pushed through, stepped up onto the escalator, with Zhuàng not far behind.

"She's not my sister. And you're not my parents, neither of you are. No matter how hard you try, repeating that same old lie over and over again isn't going to wrap the blanket of ignorance back around my eyes. You can't cover up the truth any more..."

"And what is the truth? You were offered to us, Wu. If we hadn't taken up that offer, hadn't taken on the responsibility of bringing you up ourselves, what kind of life do you think you would have had?" He planted his hand on my shoulder again as we neared the top, the steps leveling out onto the first floor, and instead of casting it off, I let it rest there for the moment.

"I don't know. But you have to understand that, until I do, until I pull out the barb and stitch up the open wound, it can never heal, and I can never truly offer forgiveness. Do you?"

Zhuàng clenched my shoulder, digging his fingers into my collarbone, before pulling it away just as we reached the end of the escalator. When he replied, walking behind while I made my way over to the security gate looming straight ahead, the emotion was choking his throat up tight enough to turn his voice hoarse. "Yes, I understand. But those days, back before you were old enough to remember them, when we fed you, clothed you, changed your nappies and cuddled you to sleep... We may not be your parents any more, not in the same way that we once were, but I promise you, whenever you need us, you will always be our son."

I stopped. Turned around, reached out to embrace the man formerly known as Dad, with the moisture starting to well up in my own eyes. Then I continued onwards, entering the maze of ropes to join the queue through security, ready to set out on the journey to find that frayed, tangled strand of my life. *Nothing would stop me from finding the answer to that question; nothing would sway me from the path I had sworn to follow to the very end...*

Lydia Keys didn't know she wanted to write until she was twenty four, when she started writing a novel, just because she felt like it. She never imagined that she could one day make a living from it! Writing is her passion, her escape, her way of seeing the world, and she wouldn't be the person she is without it.

People ask her, 'What made you think of that?' Or, 'Where do the ideas come from?' To which Lydia answers; "It's just my way of processing what's around me, kind of like a filtering process, and the written piece is the end result." Lydia Keys is 28, and currently works a full time job but she does as much writing as possible in the time she has to spare. Her short story will also be the introduction to her upcoming debut novel, **Betrayal in the Blood.**

Betrayal in the Blood

"DO NOT IMAGINE THAT THE GOOD YOU INTEND WILL BALANCE THE EVIL YOU PERFORM"

NORMAN MACDONALD

EVIL DOES NOT LURK IN DARK CORNERS; IT IS CLEAR AND PRESENT FOR ALL TO SEE. IT IS THE IGNORANCE WHICH SURROUNDS IT THAT ALLOWS IT TO THRIVE. CONSEQUENTLY IT IS ONLY WHEN WE EXPERIENCE THE INJUSTICE OF EVIL DIRECTLY, DO WE DECIDE TO RISE AGAINST IT.

The city is quiet but he cannot find his peace. Dark rain clouds form above like they did that day, shadows follow his steps like wolves stalking their prey. He was supposed to be getting married today. It was meant to be the happiest day of their lives, but he couldn't help wondering. Who was she, the baby girl on his doorstep, less than a year old? She had come with a note, it was her writing. Had he made a mistake? They had already lost so much, what would be the use in returning for another dose of pain. Every step of the way it felt as though they were swimming against the tide. She was so beautiful and he had wondered if that's what did it. Sometimes he thought it was her beauty that drove her to the edge. She didn't know what it was to be treated normally, people almost fell over themselves to be with her.

Women wanted her opinion, children wanted her love and kindness, men wanted anything she had to offer. Henry just wanted her to himself. She had told him it was out of pity that it happened, that she had felt sorry for him. She knew the effect she had on people, especially men but she couldn't understand why. No-one could explain it exactly. But in the same way that her charm and elegance attracted company, it also isolated her to the point where she was always alone. After all no-one could ever really understand what it was like.

She had come with a note:

Dearest Henry

Look what we did darling, isn't she wonderful? She is ours to keep from the rest of the world if you will hold me in your arms once more. I made a mistake, it was such a long time ago. I have not stopped loving you dear, though I hate myself for what I did, she is ours. The house is vast and empty without the sound of your voice. Sometimes I think I can see you from up here, wondering amongst the deer. They are restless without you. I write this upon the desk you made for me, do you remember Henry? A wedding gift like no other, you said. You didn't think you could offer the woman who had everything a gift but I was blessed with each day that we shared together.

I have been lost without you Henry but she has your eyes doesn't she? She has my smile. I told her to take it as I barely use mine since we parted, for the last nine months I have lived for her. If you love me darling you will bring her home to me. Bring her home Henry, please. I know you can help me get better. I will wait for three days but if I do not have you both then I must take leave for a while and you will not find me.

I wait for the day I will see you both again my love,

Eleanor

Now he carried the note in his wallet. It went with him everywhere to remind him that it hadn't been some dream, some far away fantasy that he had conjured to escape a painful memory. He wondered today if it was the right thing he was doing. Every day for the past year he had seen her begin to reflect the beauty of her Mother, the woman he abandoned then too. Every day since the note he had questioned in silence whether he should return. He had not told Nell the truth. On the third day he went there. He saw the red brick wall encircling the grounds for miles and the deer came to him at the gate. He didn't know what he was going to say or do and then he saw her. Her porcelain face at the highest window, his beautiful queen waiting for him.

She wore her hair long, the beech waves now showing flecks of grey. She was only thirty one. He could almost feel the softness of her lips upon his face, the tender strokes of her long, pale fingers. He remembered how her skin had flushed red during the first pregnancy and how she had retched at each dawn. The aching in his heart every time he reminded himself that she wasn't his. That would never go away no matter how much they loved one another, and by truth he loved her, even now. He could feel her eyes lulling him toward the large oak door but the sadness had rooted itself deep within his body and weighed down his very soul. How could he forget? Even if he went back she would never change. Eleanor would always be beautiful and even as time passed she would grace every room with her presence. He could never look straight ahead no matter how much he wanted to and she could not refuse to help people, her soul bared too much.

She would not tell him who the father was. She said the baby was a gift to him and something wonderful from a terrible mistake, but she was not theirs to keep. With the baby gone it could have been possible for Henry to forget, to move onto their future. There were moments early in the morning when he could stay lost in her maroon eyes for hours, forgetting anything that came before sunrise, but when they made love it was as though he was sharing her again. Eleanor knew he was troubled. Henry always pleased her in the most loving way but it was afterwards when he became distant that she knew they were regressing. He knew that she had been spending many hours up there where she stood today, writing. Writing what he didn't know. Her guilt had begun to slip out in her moods, some days her emotions would change in the time it took to blink. Henry was out of his depth. He could not help his queen and he could not save them. If he could forgive her she would get better, they would be free to love and live happily, but he could not live half of his life in shadows. It had been the most difficult decision of his life but he knew that if he couldn't have her to himself now then he never really had her to begin with.

Today he would do the same. He hoped that Nell would never tell his daughter the origins of her birth. What child would want to know such misery, such pain. Of course Nell didn't know she was his. Henry had been very careful about who he told his background to. The fact that he couldn't marry her was a realistic reminder that he would never be able to trust any woman again, let alone tell them what he is worth. This would be his parting gift to Nell, the child that she could never give him, even if he couldn't stay to see her grow. It is time that he stopped remembering. It is time to stop looking to the past. Today was meant to be his wedding day. Today Henry Middleton is dead.

*

She recoiled in horror. Not knowing what she was fearful of yet, she slammed the door shut hoping it would retain the information that she didn't want to know. Still, fingers of knowledge were creeping around the door frame, beckoning her closer, closer to the pain, the truth. It had hit her like a brick to the stomach, a blow to top all others. How could she have been so stupid? She sighed in contemplation, staring at the door handle. She did not know what awaited her on the other side but she knew it would change her. Everything in her being told her to turn and run, far, far away and never look back, never even speak of it, but deep within her there was a pull, an invisible cord tugging, willing her to venture through to the unknown.

Yesterday she was Nicole Singer, daughter of Jeffery and Nell Singer. Today she is adopted.

She walks, with every step she retreats further into herself, further away from the past but heading nowhere. She is inside herself, unaware that her path has led her away from the misery at number seven, Prospect Place and toward the city centre. These streets are in her blood, each one running through her veins, mapping her entire body, but she does not know. She knows she is nearing the city as the buildings grow closer to the horizon. There are three buses on the left, one is travelling to Wollaton and she thinks of her father. Her soul shrinks a little more. It was her fault that he left, because she is weak. He didn't give her a chance to fight, the voice of a child lost amongst rowing adults. What is so grown-up about them anyway? They can't agree on minor or major decisions, they don't know how to be happy and when it all gets a bit too much, they run.

She enjoys being coerced by her mind to think about something else and the feeling that her heart had imploded went away, temporarily.

The streets are crowded as she crosses Maid Marion Way and Friar Lane. There is a nightclub on the left. She doesn't understand what a nightclub is yet. She doesn't know that at three am today a couple were mugged as they left the club. She has no idea that people come here to take drugs and copulate. Nicole is ten years old, she has lived a sheltered life which only adds to the shock of what she has recently learned.

The rain beats down hard on the empty market square. It is sparse and vacant like her mind. There are too many questions, too many emotions and she has relented into her subconscious. She sits on the wide grey steps, over shadowed by the Guildhall. There are red banners hanging on either side, displaying future events in Nottingham. They waver in the swaying breeze, making them difficult to read. The fountains to her right are spraying bursts of fizzing water. It is propelled into the air, hissing, and returns with a splash into the semi still pond below. It is the only sound she can hear.

The rain is lashing at her head but she cannot feel it. She is not sheltered, from anything. She does not benefit from the warmth provided by making herself small, hugging her knees. Today she knows he is never coming back, today she is Bernadette.

I roam. I roam because I know she belongs to the city. It is her heritage, her freedom. I live within her walls and I am her citadel from the outside world, and her. She is Nicki and she will survive.

I head towards Jason's house. He will know what to do. He is a good friend and of no threat, he can protect her, love her.

His Mother answers the door. I have been walking for fifteen minutes in the rain and she makes a fuss. I am swiftly taken in, wrapped in a towel and brought in close to her. It is hard to melt into her warm embrace, but she would know something is wrong. I give her five seconds, ease back giving her a smile. "Thanks Rita," I say grinning, and then I ask for Jason.

"Yes, he's upstairs, just go on up like you always do," she says with perturbed lines across her brow. I smile again, hoping I haven't drawn too much attention to myself and quickly look to the stairs. They are carpeted in a short thread tan-brown, I learn there is cat somewhere from the long, slightly delicate fur residing there. She has built a wall around Jason, she has not entrusted me with the location of his room yet. I can't ask which room is his, it will draw suspicion. As I reach the top I am faced with a wall. The stairs and the hall make a T shape. I step to the right.

"Jase," I say, scouring the different doors. I needn't have bothered. There's a clay door hanger painted with lilac and pink fuchsias, they surround the name 'Jason'. He pokes his head around the door, my sopping feet are sinking into the spongy softness of the carpet.

"Hey you, is it raining?" He pulls the door wide open and half runs, half skips to the bay window. Drawing back the dense, black curtains, he can see for himself that it is in fact raining. The light pours in and he is illuminated. I know everything about this boy and yet I have never met him. All of that is about to change, from now on he will barely leave our side.

"He's gone." I am in a defensive position because that's what I'm doing, I'm defending. Jason is staring at me blankly.

"Who's gone?" He eventually says. I know how easily distracted he is, so I'm thinking of the quickest way to explain what has happened. We are in Jason's bedroom, which is already donning a certain feminine touch and I wonder if it is Rita's doing or his. He is sitting at the head of his bed upon a cream duvet, the bed is made and he is fluffing a pillow. "My dad," I tell him. I know that he is expecting me to break down, cry and become weak, blame myself, but I can't and I don't. My father left because he was weak, not me. I am still standing, arms crossed, waiting for Jason to say something. "Oh and I'm adopted," I almost laugh. This has his attention but he doesn't know what to say. He quickly shuffles across the bed and stands in front of me, places his hands on my shoulders. "Nic, are you ok?" He's looking me dead in the eyes, concern taking over his face. "She will be," I say.

*

She sits alone upon a single bed. It is lonely, bleak. Her room is sparse of furniture and it is plain to the eye. The lino floor is a musty yellow, she has yet to notice the scratch marks meandering from under her bed. She is missing the homely comforts of curtains, cushions and her favorite pajamas. How is it she can remember these things but she can't remember her name?

She writes:

My room is cramped and dark. The small window allows only slivers of light in through the steel bars. I do not know how I got here but I know I am missing, something. I have not seen a single mirror since I arrived here, I do not know what I will see if I happen to gaze upon one. I do not remember my achievements, if I had any but it seems I am quite good at being silent. I have not said anything to anyone, I fear I have done something wrong. Why else would I be treated this way?

****

I have loved my city, I know every dark corner and illuminated monument in this cruel place.

Snotta Inga Ham was its first name, dating back to the Saxons. It means Man Belonging Village. This was the first thing I learned, and the most important because after that, I knew I belonged to something. My father is responsible for my interest in its buildings, its character and its imprint in history; I have continued to love my city even in his absence. Although he is an architect he taught me to look past the modern distractions or obscenities as he described them, and see the life behind the structure.

I did not find it difficult to imagine the tradesmen travelling from far and wide to sell goods at the market fair. I did not struggle to visualize sinners dangling from a noose outside Shire Hall, even though it has been replaced by a Tapas bar. Every time I visit I can't help but feel outraged. How can someone build an eatery where thousands of people have perished? I make a point of scowling at anyone who goes into the building while I'm there but people just glare at me and carry on. Dad used to ask people on their way into Costa if they knew what it was before being another coffee conglomerate fogging up Britain's culture. Some of them were genuinely interested but most of them just shifted past him as quick as they could manage. Next door to Shire Hall (the gallows) is the Galleries of Justice. Contrary to the name, historical research reports scenes far from any kind of 'justice' here, but as usual the truth is embellished and sold for profit.

My connection to the city is also my connection to him but my love for it comes from somewhere far deeper. It's the way I feel when I'm breathing, the beat of my heart as I pace through its streets, the way I think I can feel its pulse. It's where I belong, with or without father.

It is not unlike any other city in that it has its crime, though it has the highest crime rate in England, with more than equal beauty to its mass, it is a fact to be easily ignored. It is a city divided into sections of love and war, the modern buildings reflecting the surge of plain work houses developed during the Industrial revolution, opposed by the delicate stone work buildings inspired by Roman architecture and later adapted by the Georgian, Edwardian and Elizabethan eras. This city had begun like any other, starting with nothing and building its way through the future. It had built upon a successful industry of wool and silk, the earliest records staring in the Middle Ages.

At the age of ten with a drunk for a mother and a lost, (not wanting to be found) father, this was the first sense of belonging I had ever known. My father never gave reason for his leaving, obviously I blamed myself. After all, what kind of ten year old is confident enough in their ability to be a perfect child wouldn't blame themselves? Now as an adult, I wish I could say that's all in the past, that I forgave myself and my father for what happened. But the truth is I am as damaged now as he must have been when he left. The feeling has never gone away, the feeling of wanting to let go of everything and everyone and start over, knowing that somehow it wouldn't be that much of a loss. I do remember those words leaving his mouth, "it's not your fault Nicole." Whenever I recall that moment it's like something's missing, like he wanted to say more but couldn't, or didn't know how to say it. Perhaps it's just normal for that particular memory to be accompanied by a severe sense of loss as that's what it was; that was the day I lost my father.

I don't remember much from that point. It was like I chose to forget as a way of blocking out anything that might provoke an emotional response. Nell had the same idea. At first she would just drink to help her sleep but soon she was sleepwalking through our lives. We were both grieving but it didn't matter. Somehow she was under the impression that a ten year old can account for themselves, that losing a husband is more hurtful than losing a father, and that I could comprehend, as an adult would, the pain we were both suffering. Or perhaps she couldn't even see through her own pain to recognize mine. I was completely alone and all I had were the streets of Nottingham. That's how I met Jason.

He was everything I wasn't, which is probably why I was so scared of him at first. I thought that if he shared, I shared and although at the time this was not a practice he forced, today he is my closest confidant. Jason was a year older than me which meant that often he acted as my crash dummy. Whenever I was too afraid to try something, (which was often) Jason would offer to check it out first. When I began having panic attacks about leaving primary school to start secondary school, Jason reassured me it would be fun, that we would see each other all of the time and that I wouldn't have to eat lunch on my own or need to make friends because I had him. He didn't make new friends either, we were two of the same, except that Jason wasn't afraid to show who he was and I hid behind him.

Life at home was still unbearable so most of the time I didn't bear it, I stayed at Jason's. Nell didn't even notice. Jason's mum began to see me as an adoptive daughter which didn't go down particularly well with his sister Beth. Fortunately Beth was hitting her teens by then and always seemed more pissed at you than she actually was, and if she was pissed at you it probably wasn't anything to do with you, but you were in the way so you got the sharp end of the stick because somebody had to. Rita was a single mum like mine but she just always seemed to cope better. It meant that Jase and I spent a lot of time in the house alone together but there was always the presence of a mother there.

There would be a meal in the slow cooker after school and Jason would wake up to his clothes laid out on the dresser ready for him. I remember thinking how Rita must have felt, coming in from a full night at the care home, sneaking into Jason's room just to make sure he had the right clothes for the next day. How kind, how thoughtful, how Motherly. At night she would tuck us both in and kiss us good night, every night.

Angel of God, my guardian dear, to whom His love commits me here. Be thy always at my side light and guide, to rule and guard.

We Thank you, for we know we are truly blessed Lord.

Until tomorrow

Amen.

Rita knew that I didn't believe in God and she knew I had my reasons, but she was also a devout Catholic. I didn't mind having the prayer said to me every night. Even when I stayed in my own bed at Nell's I found myself listening to the words in my head, surprised that I knew them so well. The truth is they comforted me. I didn't believe that anyone or anything was hearing me but I think there is comfort to be found in asking for help, no matter how subtle. I wish I could live without needing anyone. I long to switch off, give up, sleep. I wish I was strong.

I wish I could call you Mum. I know that if I call you by your name it will somehow make the pain easier to bare. It is a wall that separates us, it removes you from the space around my heart, the space I save for the ones I truly love. Part of me wishes you would find this, but deep down I know you will never care enough to read my diary, or even wonder if I have one. It's wrong Mum. It's wrong that I don't love you. It's wrong that it doesn't break my heart.

Is it possible for the place in which a person lives to transpire into the person? Perhaps I had spent too much time delving into my past; my past is Nottingham's past and I don't know if I can see where one ends and the other begins anymore. It's more than just relating to a place, I feel like I am the place and the place is me. I know every depraved, inconspicuous truth this city has to offer and I have never loved it any less.   I could never leave. I had been roaming Nottingham since I was ten years old, alone, searching for comfort within its walls.

I remember the first time I entered the Old Market Square. The Guildhall stands proudly, dominating the entire space. Even now as an adult it towers above me like a proud giant, its protecting lions proudly defend from each side. The gray flagstone tiles spread out before me, leading to the crumbly old steps of the Guildhall. The fountains to my left interfere with my peripheral sight, the water bursting out into twenty foot jets. It is familiar but every time I come here I get the same feeling; something happened here, a lot happened here but I know this affects me in a way that I can't explain. I feel like I lost something here but I can't remember what it is. How am I so attached by such a sense of loss?

I am distracted from my thoughts by children running around the shallow square pond underneath where the water is falling after being flung into the air. The hustle and bustle of street folk would normally confuse me but I'm steadied by the pure weight and intent of The Guildhall. The square is broad and long, home to goose fairs and strangers trading in the past. People would come from all over England to buy and sell.

I close my eyes. I can see brewers and bakers in dirty aprons, blacksmiths, goldsmiths and wheelwrights. They were all here to stake their claim, put their stamp on the world. The carts would begin in the old lace market and line the square. There would be hustlers, barterers, and sellers who were just trying to survive. There's always someone who struggles, always someone who just needs the bare minimum, who can only afford to look to today, not tomorrow. If they think about tomorrow they might give up hope, but they have enough hope to survive today. I know this because I have breathed Nottingham with every breath. It has the stench of survival.

I head towards Trinity Square, cross Victoria street and onto Bridlesmith. It only takes me four minutes to arrive at the Galleries. The tourist board calls it the Halls Of Justice but I know that what happened here and justice are worlds apart. Those poor people, hanged in the name of 'Justice'. A poor sinner, strung up, their family made to watch as they wave goodbye. I couldn't think of anything worse. How does that even work? In 1850 a man could be hung for stealing a loaf of bread, and today we lack a death sentence in Britain for murder. It's totally backwards. I'm not saying I agree with sentencing people to death, but where is the balance? It made my eyes well just thinking about it. It was true, Nottingham had a dark past and a lingering history to match; but however dirty and deprived it was, today it gleamed as if it were brand new, outshining the rest of the East Midlands into a shadowy shame.

I know so much about this city and yet I think I'll never

understand it. Maybe that's why I feel so comfortable in its heart and so misguided at the same time. I want my city to accept me, tell me its secrets, perhaps then I would understand my own. I know I belong here but I'm so lost.

Harry T. Greatorex studied at Exeter University and at the University of London's Birkbeck College, where he specialised in international poverty and political philosophy. As well as spending time in Latin America and Asia, he has worked with Bangladeshi communities in East London to address employment barriers and to research the impact of public policy.

An occasionally prolific songwriter and regularly stunted novelist, Harry Greatorex's short story, **O'er Both Your Houses**, addresses themes of inequality and political upheaval, and is his first piece of work to enter publication.

O'er Both Your Houses

The first gun-shots pierce the silence around the table like shards of sharp change, drawing pigment to Verona's pale cheeks and chewed pork loin from her husband's. As the glass from Maria's hand meets the tiled terracotta floor, the dark red stain spreads like the promise of a colour to come. The wide eyes of the seated couple and the standing maid meet for the first time in two long days.

Dortmand's full fork falls to his lap as his fingers grip vacantly at the air for the last trace of an evening disappeared. Six courses strewn across the table now seem a world apart. He pushes past his maid in his haste to drag the heavy dining room doors together and fumbles in his pocket for the key. Maria falls back against the wall as he passes, one hand grasping at the high windowsill for balance.

Footsteps on the stairs and a strangled barking from the courtyard bring Verona to her feet and her hands together, knuckles whitening to match the linen table-cloth.

The key!

Voices in the hall and the sound of doors slamming open against the wood finish. They are at the landing now.

The key!

Dortmand fishes deeper as menace seeps blindly under the great doors. Silence in the hall like a held breath. Footsteps again, but much softer. Dortmand kneels, still groping, panting prayers between fast-clenched teeth.

The distance from the pocket to the keyhole is nothing. Metal scrapes hidden metal as the bolt tumbles home and Dortmand falls back on his haunches, stifling sucked-in breaths with a palm soon slick with saliva.

*

A trail of dust from the jungle road followed Jeremiah as he climbed the staircase to the landing. He paused momentarily to catch his breath and to take in again the wealth of his surroundings. Rare glimpses of Herr Dortmand's private rooms in seventeen years of distant servitude had stoked the imagination, working their way in front of his age-old ambitions until they submerged them completely.

Only one house in the village had two floors, let alone the grand, endless staircase of the mansion. The German family had ruled the *pueblita* at the edge of the jungle for as long as anyone could remember. The house dominated the landscape, its opulence scorning Lenin's doctrine. A doctrine whispered in the backroom of the bakery for too long. Jeremiah kept moving.

Pressing the heel of one stained-red hand to his good eye, Jeremiah forced the memory of young gate-keep's frightened tears from his mind. Like the rest, the boy's hollow cheeks had sucked no life from the unforgiving courtyard-slabs. The gaps in the stone work had drunk so greedily from the bullet wound in his chest. In an ornate frame at the top of the staircase, Jeremiah's eyes stared past the surface of the painting, seeing only the poor boy's end.

That, then, was the price. Half a lifetime of carefully placed whispers had peaked in two short days of feverish inaction and now this. He continued up the staircase, able to spare the lush carpets of his bile only while he kept moving.

In his clutch; the drooping pistol. He prayed it would have no further use. Jeremiah tracked Dionisio to the landing where, legs braced wide, the farmer's strength competed with ancient lock and timber. The white shirt stretched taught against his shoulders was stained with old sweat from the field and fresh blood from the courtyard. As the fading light from the stained-glass window played across his soaking back, it was impossible to tell the colour of war from that of the harvest.

The ancient double-doors loomed tall and heavy to the carved cornice where the ceiling began, their simple finish out of place against the detail of the fine-papered walls. They were the first thing Jeremiah had seen in the house that was of the land here. Most of the lavish decorations no doubt hailed from some far off country where skilled craftsmen toiled to meet the demands of far-flung colonial heroes. Even the power in Dionisio's hands, fuelled full as <u>it</u> <u>was</u> by hot pride and shame, offered no match for the aged Amazonian timber.

"They are inside?"

"*Si*. Two at least."

"And Maria?"

Dionisio looked at the floor.

"*Si.*"

Dionisio turned now to face his new comrade. Jeremiah's thick stubble stretched to his shirt collar where day-old flour stains belied his recent graduation from baker to butcher. He moved uncertainly across the polished floorboards to join Dionisio and ran both hands over the wood, gauging the thickness.

"An axe?"

The farmer shook his head and spoke softly.

"If he has a pistol, we lose whoever breaks through."

Jeremiah nodded at this and took a step away from the doors, his eyes drifting to the keyhole near his waist.

"We burn them, then."

Dionisio shook his head again. "The roof would catch first, *hermano*. Perhaps the jungle too. It hasn't rained in three months." He leant against the door frame now, the words snatched between heavy breaths. This was the first respite since the tense meeting in the kitchen at the bakery. A meeting that had spilled into decision for the first time in twenty years of harboured grudges and hushed mutterings. Mutterings that Dionisio had always dismissed as the vain talk of lazy men.

Both men tensed on the landing as the muffled sound of renewed fighting reached them from the floor below. Dionisio held out his hand for the pistol and Jeremiah passed the weapon wordlessly. The farmer checked the chamber of the revolver and leveled the barrel at the top of the staircase as Jeremiah fought the urge to move behind his comrade.

*

At Maria's feet, fractured glass distorts the tiles beneath and reflects the ceiling above, where heat-dazed fruit flies stalk their reflections among the flaccid stalagmites of a forgotten chandelier. Blood drips unnoticed from the cut on Maria's hand, the loud spots stretching desperate fingers across her starched apron.

The flies have descended now, orbiting the food on the table in a sleepy rhythm. Verona moves a trembling hand through the silence to correct the position of her cutlery on her dinner plate: the meal is over.

Still Dortmand kneels, prone, in front of the double doors as whoever, whatever, is outside tests their ancient strength again.

Now soft voices beyond, muffled through timber to distort all but their urgency. Dortmand's wife and maid watch as their patriarch sits back on fat haunches, ragged snorts of breath forcing out from between soft fingers.

After a moment, he stands, swaying heavily, and turns to face the women in his life. Maria, the girl who in but two months has achieved the ruin that Verona, in seventeen years of cold disdain and spite had failed to bring about. This much seems clear now.

He trudges the seven steps to the cabinet, opening the drawer and taking out the small, silver pistol that has never been fired. A single round rolls in the dark as the drawer opens, the sound splitting the silence between the three.

"The men from the guardhouse will surely..." begins Verona, trailing off as her husband slams the drawer closed. He quietly wipes his face with his shirtsleeve before returning to his place at the head of the table. He places the pistol next to his plate and begins to tear pork from the bone with his fingers.

As the sound Dortmand's appetite fills the room, Maria closes her eyes tightly and waits for her father.

*

Below stairs, the crash of breaking furniture was punctuated by the firecracker-pop of Old Luis' hunting rifle. A pause, and Old Luis' frantic panting issued up the staircase, the faint note of panic quickly swallowed up by the towering ceilings.

"*Esta bien, esta bien*," Luis called up to Jeremiah. "It was only the kitchen hand, Javier. His confirmation would have been next summer... not anymore, not anymore."

"He's dead?" called Jeremiah, reaching to Dionisio to take the pistol again. "I... I know his mother."

"Not dead, dying," shouted Old Luis. Then more quietly, to Javier, "Softly, *hermano*. Not long for this world."

On the landing, the two men listened as Luis kicked his way across the broken furniture in the dining room below to reach the boy.

"So many..." choked Jeremiah, "I never knew they had so many..."

"Servants?" asked Dionisio, evenly. "But of course. We all are."

Jeremiah's swoon was interrupted as he rested a sweating hand on the solid wooden doors. *His* wooden doors now, or **surely** very soon. The old man would **surely** give up without much more of a fight. Lord only knew how the sullen landowner had inspired such loyalty among the men they had fought as they breached the house.

The guard in the conservatory had been the worst. The boy had hardly made a sound as he struggled in vain between the unforgiving wall and Dionisio's strength. The farmer had forced the point of his knife up under the young man's chin to end his days, blotting out the sun setting through the glass with the sudden spray of gore.

Dionisio had turned to Jeremiah then, blinking the man's blood from his eyes like a child's tears.

And now the great doors were all that stood between them and the final confrontation.

"Perhaps they will open them?" suggested Jeremiah, raising his fist to knock on the wood and pausing as he thought better of it.
"Would you?" asked Dionisio.

Jeremiah smiled the wide smile of the groundsman who, in a moment of sudden rationality, realises the snake in the grass is far more frightened of him than he of it.
"Then we wait."

*

Only when Verona's muffled sobs have slowed to show sleep does Maria dare sneak bread and water from the table. She selects the crusts and scraps from the baker's best, avoiding the remains of the meat now busy with flies. No choice but to use the fine white china, she blushes in the dark and glances at her master. Dortmand's head is in his hands, his shirtsleeve dragging the remains of his meal across the table. Juice from the meat bleeds into wine spilt by sleeping fingers.

She is sore from standing for so long and sorer still from her master's appetite. Maria moves through the shadowed room with held breath, ignoring the pistol where it lies on the tablecloth, liberated by sleep.

The key!

The key sits in the lock, forgotten by her slumbering employers. Maria, heavy with shame, retires to a corner with her meal, her apron wrapped around her shoulders against the night. Through silent tears, she watches a spider crawl to freedom between cracks in the window frame and waits for her father.

*

By morning, the rest of the house had been searched and the evening's tension had evaporated with the dew. The jungle lay sleeping in three directions where the gardens finished, birdcall silenced by something very different on the wind.

Verona had been discovered in the dusty flower bed beneath the dining room window at daybreak. Busy ants trailed from bleeding nose to gaping mouth, locked as it was in a final scream that none had heard, even in the quiet of night. Her limbs had been curiously twisted by the fall, as if the wind had plucked her from the high ledge above and blown her to Caracas and back, petticoats billowing above the tree-tops.

Only one more of Dortmand's men had been found. He had pleaded softly in blood-stained German between the punches as two brothers from the village had taken turns in the moonlight. He was eventually drowned in the

horse-trough, his last words bubbling to the surface of the murky water without translation.

Dionisio had discovered the scene at the finish, the back of his hand soon leaving its mark on his two comrades for their efforts. The men had glared at one another, smarting in silence, as each dared the other to challenge the farmer. Something unfinished in Dionisio's eyes seeded fear in the men and soon won their compliance.

Jeremiah had Old Luis move Dortmand's desk and chair from his study to set up on the landing. He sat in the master's chair, exploring the workings of the pistol with his fingers and waiting for victory. He took his breakfast outside the double doors while his men strolled from room to room, ransacking delicacies from the pantry and pondering the silver candlesticks they all knew were locked in the dining room.   Dionisio, his back tired from a night on hard floorboards, had them drag the bodies outside, leaving them lined up in the shade to await last rites.

"They are *ladrones*, comrade. *San Pedro* will reject them," one man complained, now tired twice by the killings.

"They are sons and brothers, *hermano*," said Dionisio. "And it is *San Pedro* who will decide."

Dionisio was learning the power of movement. If he kept busy, kept working as he always had, then the dining room and its occupants were just another task for tomorrow. He found work to be done and did not pace the landing with Jeremiah, or cup a glass to the wood like Old Luis. Contained within were the answers to a question too painful for all his strength to carry.

Night had brought no rest for Dionisio, his sleep had been broken and unforgiving. He had found a dark corner of the study and balled up like a wounded animal, only the wound was rumour and the animal had a temper. The story of what the grocer's wife had seen in the south fields had spread through the marketplace like the pox. Indeed, such was the scandal that talk turned from the spread of plague for the first time in so many weeks.

How proud Dionisio had been when Maria had first been taken up to the house to meet Dortmand's people. Fine work for a young woman, work that might spare her the stoop and strain of the fields for a few years at least. Not anymore, not anymore.

Jeremiah had heard the story and wasted no time. Every revolution needs a man of action and in Dionisio, hands blistered and grained from hoe and shovel, the village might yet have their own. Herr Dortmand was not a cruel master, but master he was. And as they waited, unexpectant for some happening to break the rhythm from below stairs, now came this from above that could not be ignored.

They all knew what tricks could be conjured by the jungle mist rising in the heat of the morning, but whether truth or fantasy now made little difference. A young girl's virtue came above law, above fear. There was reason now. Reason other than Jeremiah's greed for carpets and high ceilings and, dare he think it, for servants of his own.

As the sun rose above the trees, the house creaked and groaned as men awoke and floorboards gave up the night's moisture to the breeze.

"How long can they last?" asked Jeremiah between mouthfuls. He ate with one hand, the pistol aimed lazily at the double doors, his boots crossed on the desk in front of him.

Dionisio shrugged. "They could have food and water for several days," said the farmer, who had visited the kitchen after his comrades and could make no measure from what they had left untouched- if a meal had been taken above stairs at all.

Jeremiah snorted at this, discarding a chicken bone onto his plate and licking his fingers clean. Only with Dortmand dead would the house be his. One more body, or two, would signal the end of it all.

"Several days with your daughter," said Jeremiah slowly, watching Dionisio's eyes drop to the floor as the words hit home like hammer blows. "We cannot allow this, comrade, for her sake."

Dionisio's fists clenched until the knuckles whitened under the blood stains. Jeremiah's greed was all around them, from the bodies under the trees to the broken furniture and bullet holes the kitchen. Men too young to know the meaning of loyalty had killed and been killed for masters old and new. Years of humble obedience thrown away to feed the baker's hunger for power and prestige.

All this was dwarfed by Dionisio's shame. Shame that in his pride he had hoped for more for his daughter and his family. Shame for what harm had come to Maria and shame that even now, in the light of morning, his fears had stayed his hand.

As Dionisio stepped forward, the harlequin light from the stained-glass played once again across his features. In one movement he snatched the pistol from Jeremiah's hand by the barrel and gripped the edge of the desk with the other. Long-tired muscles strained as Dionisio lifted the desk, spilling Jeremiah scrambling across the floorboards as he smashed the desk into splinters against the great double doors. Grazed and shaken from the fall, Jeremiah recoiled as Dionisio strode towards him. The farmer, moving with purpose, ignored his fallen general and marched down the staircase, leaving Jeremiah alone, panting on the landing.

*

Maria wakes at the noise outside to see Dortmand standing over her, malice in his eyes and fists in his hands. Even with her view blocked by her master's bulk she can sense they are now alone. The curtains billowing from the half-opened window entwine with the heavy chair, dragged from its place at the foot of the table in the dead of night.

Maria presses herself further into the skirting and wraps her apron yet tighter around her shoulders. Dortmand leans in and grips her throat with a hand sticky with pork and sweat, the other fumbling, fumbling at his belt buckle. His breath is on her hot and heavy as she struggles, reaching with frantic fingernails to scratch his face, her thin wrists punched aside as he staggers back, then comes in again.

Dortmand starts to cough once more, his convulsions wracking both bodies as his weight bears down on his maid. He spits in Marias face and wipes the last of it back across the furious red marks on his cheek. He grabs her hair and dashes her head against the wall, leaving a fresh stain on the flaking paper. Dragging Maria from the corner and turning her over, Dortmand removes his belt. The girl thrashes now, sobs pouring over. He binds Maria's wrists behind her, pulling the leather tight until she gasps at the pain. He pulls her, still struggling, to the chair, wrestling with his coughing and the curtain alike as he lifts her to sit facing the doors.

Maria chokes back tears as blood warms her forehead and mattes into her hair. She fixes her eyes on the double doors as Dortmand fishes the silver pistol from his waistband, moves behind her and rams the barrel hard into the back of her neck.

*

Dionisio cleared the staircase and pushed past Old Luis in the hall, his ears deaf to Jeremiah's shouts from the landing. The hunter moved aside as the farmer passed, looking to the kitchen and his rifle lying loaded on the table. Dionisio hurried through the blood-stained conservatory and out to the courtyard where the brothers from the village were stoking a fire with broken furniture and books they could not read. They watched him pass silently, their eyes following the pistol in his hand.

Through the dying gardens, Dionisio ran past stumps of European shrubs, long defeated by sun and scorched earth. He stamped through flowerbeds choked with native vines where skeletal hedgerows wilted into the soil. He snatched a hoe from the ground and levered the storeroom door, the aged wood splintering easily to give up the lock. Inside, Dionisio tossed aside cobwebbed tools, unearthing ancient rakes and shears long rusted by the jungle air.

Outside, Dionisio moved on across sun-bleached lawns to the servants' quarters, his eyes searching constantly for the axe. The building squatted in the shade where the jungle spilt over into the garden, darker still where flies swarmed busily from a broken window.

Dionisio slowed now, looking for signs that the building had been searched as he had asked and finding none. Shouts now, from the direction of the house. He gripped the hoe tighter and edged forward, drawing the pistol with his free hand.

As he reached the door, Dionisio was hit hard by the rank smell of decay. The hoe fell from his fingers and he dropped to his knees beside it. His head span, full suddenly of the last strangled pleas of the German they had drowned in the horse trough. On the wooden door a chalk cross was marked tall and clear against the grain.

*

Dortmand doubles up, dropping to one knee at the pain. His lungs are itching now inside his chest, their crimson spores peppering his shirt sleeve as he covers his mouth with the back of his wrist as he coughs. One hand on the belt at Maria's back and the other on the pistol leave his stance is twisted, unbalanced, so that each rocking cough threatens to spill him across the floorboards.

"Listen to me," says Maria, at last, addressing her master through

blood and tears. "Listen to me."

The words have a quiet strength that her tired body has never carried.

"It is over, Master. One way or another." She speaks softly, feet finding floorboards as she rises from her chair, tugging the leather belt gently from Dortmand's grasp and backing slowly across the room to the corner. She feels the commotion through the floorboards from the rooms below, sits, and watchers her master gasping for breath in the light from the window.

*

"Stop -listen! We don't need to… *hermanos*, listen! The farmer is crazy with grief.'

But the men toiled on, sweating wordlessly as the sun rose in the sky.

"This is madness," pleaded Jeremiah, panting in the midday heat as he watched the men pile the bodies one by one back into the house. Warm again from sun, limbs dangling from their sockets, the corpses were carried to the conservatory, boots and fingers dragging in the dust as they went.

"Now firewood," said Dionisio, his voice muffled through the torn shirt-sleeve tied around his nose and mouth. The men nodded and went about their duties, eyes narrowed as they pushed past Jeremiah where he stooped now, fishing for china in the kitchen.

"Everything stays, Jeremiah," said Dionisio. "We cannot risk it. Nothing escapes the pox. I have half a mind to kill us all and chalk the doors. But then," He pulled his General around to face him. "I never was a man for violence."

Jeremiah looked on as the men shattered chairs and cabinets for kindling, arranging the pieces around the bodies and the skirting. He followed Dionisio from room to room, as the farmer tore pages from great leather-bound volumes to litter the carpets and stuff into crevices.

"But your daughter," said Jeremiah at last. "You must surely think of Maria."

Only now did Dionisio stop and look to the ceiling above. He removed his handkerchief and turned to Jeremiah, wet tracks of tears shining through the sweat and dirt on his face.

"Think of my daughter?" said Dionisio. "But I have done nothing else." The farmer turned now to Old Luis, waiting patiently with match and lamp oil. "You may light the fires. I am sure Lenin would approve."

Once outside, the men rested in the shade, listening to the bellow of the flames as the curtains caught and the fire stalked through the grand building. They drank quietly, whispered fearfully, and waited to see if the flames reached the jungle.

Originally from Leicester, **Ben Wright** is 21 years old, and has spent the last 3 years at Bristol University. This June, he completed his degree (Bsc Geography) and after having left the embrace of student life, finds himself thrust into the daunting but exciting prospect of searching for a career. Though a scientist by trade, he's more of an artist by nature, and loves being creative – either through painting/drawing, or playing the guitar.

Perhaps his biggest passion is writing. Ben Wright has always written stories and has long had dreams – like most would-be authors – of seeing his work in print. Some of his favourite authors are Iain Banks, Carlos Ruiz Zafon, and Tolkien, and he often finds himself drawing influence from their works. Ben Wright's ultimate dream is to have a book of his own on the shelf, and hopefully, this short story, **The Woman of the Tower**, and its inclusion as part of this anthology, will be the first few steps towards that!

The Woman of the Tower

I'm on my way to Starbucks and dreading it. Yes, there is something slightly sinister about them, but it's not that. It's the people who I'm due to meet in this particular Starbucks.

Catching up with old friends always splits me. Either I really look forward to reminiscing and everything flows as if we'd never travelled down different roads for a time, or... things couldn't be more awkward. The conversation is strained, the smiles forced, the glances at watches real and hopeful.

And I'm fearful this encounter will slip into the latter category. And it's not Joel – I mean, he only went down to Southampton for six months to work, and we are good friends with plenty to talk about. The thing is, this time... May will be there.

The ironic thing is I've known May for far longer than I have Joel. Joel and I met close to ten years ago now, when I first seriously entered the writer's world. He gave me my first 'break', if you could call it that. His father was then editor for a local arts magazine that occasionally featured poems and short stories.

'*Show me some of your stuff and I'll see what I can do*,' he'd said in the White Hart, where we met. I can't say it was how I had envisaged my first publication – a three thousand word piece in a Mag with around forty regular subscribers. But someone liked what they read, and things took off from there. Spluttered off the ground, at least. So I owe quite a bit to Joel.

May – his wife of only two years – and I, go back to college. We took our A-levels together. We could have shared something else if things had worked out. I just never really got her... full stop, if you want to be crude. But, what I mean is, I never felt like I knew where

I stood. We could be chatting like friends, joking, laughing, and then our eyes would meet and there would be something there. And I would feel like saying something, but never did, because of those other times. The times when she passed by me in the corridor with her fiends without so much as a hello, or even a smile, the occasional awkward silence, the glances at others that I had thought and secretly wished were only for me. I felt like I was being led on and was tired of it. I didn't see her again after the summer exams in our final year, and wasn't sorry for it... much.

So imagine my shock – not quite horror, but not far off – when Joel finally introduces me to the girl he's been seeing and singing the praises of for the last few months, the girl it was getting 'pretty serious' with. In he walks, into our usual haunt, the Hart, and following him a small unwanted slice of my history. My heart skipped a little nonetheless; I instantly knew it was her, and was immediately reminded why I had felt the way I did about her. Her mucky blonde hair was wavy, messy in a tamed way, resting on her shoulders. She looked as if she hadn't gained a pound since A-levels – more than could be said for myself – and save for some harsher lines under her eyes and around her mouth, could well have walked in on the way back from college.

I felt myself shrinking away from Joel's searching gaze, but couldn't avoid his eye as he scanned the pub. He grinned and turned to May, pointing over to my corner as he did so. I felt a lurch in my stomach as she looked over to where I sat, but her expression didn't change. I heard myself laugh cynically – just like her to fail to recognise me.

I saw the new look in her eyes as she came closer, the realisation of who this figure was, shrouded in the gloomy light against the far wall. She let out a small smile and a brief nod of acknowledgment as Joel 'introduced' us.

"I know," she said, and explained to a confused Joel. I got the feeling neither of us wanted to talk about 'old times' or ask what the other had been doing with their lives since. But Joel took some time to calm down – not in anger, but in bewilderment – over the fact that his girlfriend and best friend had been acquainted without his knowledge. So he naturally wanted to dig up all that had happened between us. May summed it up – *We were just friends really*. And I smiled and nodded, and mercifully, the topic of conversation changed.

They were getting married. I let out a cough of horrified surprise, and did my best to make it seem natural and unrelated to the crazy words that had just come out of Joel's mouth. He was grinning wildly, first at me, and then at May, who smiled back with a smile I immediately knew was filled with genuine love. I stopped myself from saying what I felt sensible, and tried to phrase it in a more appropriate way.

"You didn't hang around, did you?" Suffice to say I've never been a great speaker – writing always gives me that little bit more time, allowing me to make less of a fool of myself. But they didn't seem to take it in offense.

"Why wait when everything's perfect?" Joel said happily, placing his hand on May's.

Perfect indeed. From then on, whenever I saw Joel I tried to make it something or somewhere where May wouldn't join us. It sounds cruel, I know – even spiteful – but there was always something unspoken between us, and the tension I just hate – I'm quite awkward enough thank you.

So now they've been married for two years, and are back

having spent the last six months in Southampton, where Joel worked as assistant editor to a city-wide paper.

I suppose this is to be a harmless catch up, but I can't rid of me this ominous feeling, a foreboding of something huge, crushing –

Ah. Okay, calm down – six months is a long time and people change. But no. As I wave back to the couple walking down on the opposite side of the road, it's a feeble and vain hope that May has simply let herself go.

The traffic lights are red. The cars stop. They walk over and down towards me. Joel is grinning as usual; May is smiling too, in a slightly sheepish way.

"Well," I begin, honestly with no way of finishing the sentence.

"Shall we go in?" Joel suggests. I nod in agreement. May walks in first, hands on bump, and Joel puts his arm out.

"After you."

Inside, May is standing at the wrong end of a rather long queue. The tables are all occupied. It is hot and bustling in here. I see her cast an exasperated look at Joel, who smiles and shrugs. She frowns at him – that was not the right response.

"It's too busy," she says definitively. "We'll have to go somewhere else."

"Oh, we'll find somewhere here," Joel replies airily – the wrong tone I judge (correctly). "People are bound to leave."

May clutches his arm. "I want to find somewhere else– it's too busy."

Joel is sensible enough not to argue further, and looks at me apologetically. "Um, let's try somewhere else, shall we? Sorry about that."

"No worries."

I follow the two of them back out onto the noisy street, and we head down the hill to the next coffee shop, all of fifty metres away. We walk in.

"That's more like it," May declares, appearing much calmer.

"Right, you two find somewhere to sit, and I'll get us all a drink," Joel says genially to us, completely unaware of the dread he has caused us, at the prospect of spending a few minutes alone without his easing presence.

Joel goes over to the counter, leaving May and me looking anywhere but at each other.

"After you," I say, hoping she'll just sit down somewhere and I can follow. We sit down next to a large Degas print, both staring longingly at Joel as he pulls out a ten, watching the girl take a cup to the filter machine.

We're sitting in silence and I feel like laughing. How ridiculous is this? And I don't even know why or how it ended up like this. Perhaps she can simply sense my awkwardness. I do have a rather gifted ability of bringing an uncomfortable air with me, no matter what the situation. It's as if it rubs off on people. I suppose that's why I get on with Joel so well – he's so easy to be around, not to mention making being around other people a stroll in the park.

With an almost audible sigh of relief, I watch him walk over and place the tray before us. He sits down and takes a sip. Still he hasn't said anything – no one has. I imagine saying something about an elephant in the room, but it probably wouldn't be very considerate.

"So, how are things going?" Joel asks.

"Yeah, good," I reply with my usual.

"Really?"

"Well, I suppose I'm in a bit of a rut at the moment, but it'll pick up again, I'm sure." I hope he's talking about writing, as I am, and not my life in general. True as my summary may be, I wouldn't feel comfortable disclosing my melancholy state. I'll have to make it obvious it's writing I'm talking about.

"It's a cliché, but I just need some inspiration, really."

"You could do with a muse," suggests Joel, grinning boyishly. "How goes things on that front?"

It's as if May isn't even here to him, and I get the impression she is beginning to feel the same way. I can't say I'm comfortable talking about this in front of her, mainly because I don't want her to know how sorry and desperate it's been recently.

"Well, quiet I suppose, but then I'm not really looking," I say extremely unconvincingly. Perhaps I don't even want to convince them.

"Not looking?" Joel raises an eyebrow. "That's not a good sign. You don't want to start getting comfortable. But there's plenty of time."

I shudder, looking at Joel – someone I had thought (and ashamedly hoped) more unlikely than me to get married – and his wife of two years, and their unspoken unborn child.

"Of course there is," I say with a smile, but I'm not able to pull back the cynicism from my voice, and Joel catches it.

"Right," he declares alarmingly, placing his mug down on the table, staring at me with a serious smirk on his face. "Before we leave this cafe, you're going to go up to the girl behind the counter and ask for her number."

I laugh. "Sure, okay."

"I'm incredibly serious."

I take a hurried glance over to the counter – behind the safety of my coffee-mug – and spy a slim red-head through the line of customers. I turn back to Joel, who still has that infuriating smirk etched on his face.

"No, I don't think–"

"Go on. Do it."

"Well, maybe." It's as non-committal as it's possible to be, but Joel clings to it.

"Hey, there you go chief – back in the game."

I shake my head chuckling at Joel's persistence but safe in the knowledge that I have no intention of asking for the girl's number.

I look at May, feeling someone ought to bring her into the conversation, even if I'm happy her being outside it. But as I do, I see her exchange a look with her husband and suddenly something changes.

Joel clears his throat, takes a sip of coffee, and clears his throat again. May watches him impatiently. I feel incredibly tense with no idea why.

"You've probably noticed a little bit of a change in May's appearance," he began, tearing at the edges of a napkin and offering the occasional fleeting glance in my direction. "Guilty as charged, I'm afraid."

"That's fantastic – congratulations!"

They both smile. "Thanks mate," Joel replies, but that's not all, I can tell. "And, well... Both May and I... We've been discussing it, and..." (Oh man, I think I know) "...We'd love it if you would be the kid's Godfather."

After the suited, shrouded figure of Vito Corleone flashes in and out of my mind, I realise what Joel is actually saying. If something, *God forbid*, should happen to the two of them, then they want and trust me – *me* – to take on the role of parent to their child, to love and look after it as if it was my own. *How on earth* did they end up deciding on me? Out of all the people Joel – and May especially – knows, they can think of no one better, no one more suited, no one better experienced *than me*? Inside I'm cracking up with the absurdity of it; they must be mad. But then I calm down – it is only a theoretical situation after all, an honorary title. It means nothing, unless the worst happens... and when does that ever really happen? It just doesn't, not in my life. So just say it – make them happy.

"Of course. How could I say no?" Just an honorary title. It means nothing.

"Excellent!" Joel exclaims, smiling at May, who smiles down into her mug.

"So... do you know when it's due?" I ask, hoping May will answer.

"About six weeks," Joel answers. "Kind of scuppered our summer plans, but I won't hold it against the little scamp."

"Do you know what it'll be?"

Joel shakes his head, an uncontrollable look of excitement on his face. "No, we both decided we wanted to wait." He looks over to May, who beams back, stroking her bump affectionately. I can feel envy's spiked horns jabbing in my chest, but at this moment, it seems to be wrapped in the softening strait-jacket of genuine warmth; I am truly happy for them.

We spend the next half an hour simply talking, about what we've been doing, about the present state of things (are they ever good?). May says little, but I get the impression she is more comfortable. Maybe being close friends again isn't such a stretch of the imagination.

We are about to leave. Joel is holding the door open for May. As I pass through he suddenly grips my arm and gives me a look that I immediately shake my head to.

"You almost got away with it, didn't you?" he says coyly.

"No, forget it, Joel," I protest, trying to ease myself out into the pavement.

"*Ababab*, not so fast. You said you would remember?"

"I think I said maybe."

"I heard yes."

"Well you need to get your ears checked."

"Fine, fine." Joel relinquishes his grip. "Just go and thank her for the coffee. Say it was really nice, thank you." His wide brown eyes dare me, like a nervous teenager goading another on. He won't back down – I know him too well.

"Okay," I finally concede, feeling the butterflies festering in my stomach already. I'm a grown man, for Goodness' sake – you'd think I'd be over this stage by now.

As I walk back to the counter, as if this were my death march, I see the girl clearly for the first time, and wonder what the hell I'm doing.

She looks young. Blemishless skin, taught over high cheekbones, a small pointed nose, an elegant neck showing from underneath her fiery hair, pulled over her shoulders to fall down her back.

I'm standing in the queue with two people ahead of me. To my left, behind the counter, is the large filter machine, and its shiny metal exterior shows me a tired face covered in dirty-looking stubble and hair that wouldn't know what to do with itself, even if there was slightly more of it.

Glancing over my shoulder, I see the couple outside on the pavement, their backs turned, seemingly chatting to each other. I think I've stood here long enough to convince him, and convince myself of other things. I've also no doubt saved myself embarrassment, an awkward stutter and a polite, humouring smile.

I leave my position and go over to join Joel and May. Joel turns as I come out of the cafe, his custom grin easily taking its usual position.

"Well?"

"Oh, I just said thank you, and she smiled and said thank you back."

"There you go," Joel responds brightly, apparently taking my drivel. "Now, next time, she'll recognise you as that nice, polite guy with the charming smile."

I nod. "Basically, I'm in then?" I look at May. She's smirking at her shoes, what she can see of them anyway.

Lilly Roberts is presently studying Creative Writing with the Open University, where she took on a degree for personal achievement rather than her career prospects. Through this, she has grown as an unexpected writer.

Although in her professional life she has always worked in the care industry, Lilly Roberts has always enjoyed writing stories, and has many anecdotes from over the years. **Touched by War** was her final piece of her third year course, and she hopes to continue its steady development into a novel.

Touched By War

Jane sipped her home made lemonade and sighed as the warm summer breeze caressed her cheeks.

'You're right though, it is stunning,' she said gazing down the valley.

The valley gave a comforting static view that varied through the drama of the seasons. A dark cloud loomed on life's horizons that would change the valley for good.

'Shame the rest of the world isn't as peaceful,' she said to Daniel, her husband. The years of farm work had been kind to him, apart from furrows of worry mapped out on his forehead.

She watched as his expression changed, aware he was thinking of the times ahead. The war had been on-going for over a year and the death toll was rising. If those Lord Kitchener posters were right soon all men would be needed for King and Country, she was sure of it.

'What will you do if I'm conscripted?' he said cringing. It was a situation neither of them wanted to talk about. Jane held his gaze as she reached forward to touch his face.

'Sweetheart, I will survive... and so will you.'

He kissed her and held her tight. They had been married for fifteen years and together their love and strength had grown. As Jane stared at him, she knew he would do anything asked of him, as he was honourable, but like most women at this time, she took second seat after King and Country. She sat on his lap in the rocking chair as he rocked, she couldn't think about the war, she was so happy, so content, no one should be able to take this away. They watched the distance as Lilly, their ten year old daughter danced up the hill, kicking the summer flowers as she practiced her ballet moves. Meg, her collie, weaved in and out of her legs, tripping her up and then jumping on her.

'Look, here comes trouble. You entertain your daughter while I cook dinner,' she said, ruffling his hair and disappearing inside.

The front door opened onto a small hall, filled with shelves stacked with boots and shoes and a jumbled mess of seasonal coats. This small space opened into the main living area, a large room filled with beautiful heavy wooden furniture. At one end a small double bed, partitioned off from the room with a magnificent red velvet curtain. Above this area overhung an old hay loft or balcony that now comprised of just a bed. Lilly called this space her indoor tree house and she loved it. She had watched her father as Daniel had constructed timber walls to give her privacy. The other room was smaller, situated out the back, with a spare double bed and a wood burner in the corner, this was for guests.

Jane's favourite place in her simple home was at the other end of the room, a tall, grand inglenook fireplace that took up most the wall and where Jane created delicious meals that their purse strings allowed. Her passion for cooking always lingered in the air. Today, the smell of fresh baked bread and scones wafted out of the open window. The aromas from the hunger crunching smell of a delicious dinner filled her nostrils with delight, making her mouth water in anticipation. As Jane tended to the hoggart stew on the stove, she listened to her daughter and husband playing, winding up Meg so much so she sounded like she was choking on her own bark.

Mr Humphreys from the village had the ability to arrive at the right moment. It was as if he could smell her baking from two miles away and appeared just as they were warm enough to be devoured. She heard Dolly, the old horse's heavy breathing, like she was complaining about the steep hill with a heavy load on such a warm day. Jane looked out to see Lilly running to fetch water and carrots, Dolly snorted a response. Mr Humphreys grunted and groaned as he lowered himself to the ground. He was a portly gentleman, owner of the grocery store, so knew everyone and their business. As Jane looked out the window she watched him bounce his way towards the house, his face swollen and red resembling a large beetroot and he sniffed the air, smiling and licking his lips ready to feast on her fresh baked delights.

'Good evening Mr Humphreys, come and sit down in the shade here. I'll fetch you some fresh lemonade.' She shuffled the chair into the shade on the porch, it creaked with the excess weight it now supported as Mr Humphreys flopped down.

'Why thank you my dear,' Mr Humphreys gasped for breath through his restricted diaphragm. 'It is a little hot today. Your scones smell heavenly, distracting a man from his worries. Any chance of a small sample?' He smiled and fanned himself with his hat while Jane fetched them scones.

'Now tell me of the news in the village?' she asked, knowing he was desperate to have a good gossip.

'Jane my dear, the war continues.' He paused to catch his breath a while and finish off the sweet citrus drink. 'The village hall is being set up for men to sign up, time for the young folk to be conscripted.' Jane's legs wobbled under her as the colour drained from her face. She knew that the time had come.

*

A few days later, everybody in the village and throughout the

Somerset valley was buzzing about the news. Young men signing up to go and fight for King and Country, others like Daniel, conscripted. They walked to the enlisting office as a family, they both knew that at some point soon, they would be separated for the first time since they met. Jane's silent tears glistened on her cheek as she watched her brave husband sign the recruitment form. Without a word, they began their way back to the farm to enjoy what little time they had left.

Those days rapidly depleted, time was not on their side and only a short while later they had his signature. Daniel packed a small amount of belongings into a bag. There was a heavy atmosphere in the room as Lilly scowled and wept at her father.

'Daddy, please wait until the war comes here and then fight the bad people. Why do you have to go away?' she wailed as she stared at her father.

'Lilly sweetheart, I don't have a choice. This is orders of the King.' He touched her cheek and wiped away her tears. 'You need to be strong and help your mother around the farm.'

'When will you be back?' she looked up at her father with big brown sad eyes.

'Hopefully before Christmas,' he said holding her tight. Jane knew everyone hoped for that as she watched through the open door. The tightening of her throat muscles made it hard to swallow and breathe, she couldn't quite believe that he had to leave. Daniel stood there in his uniform, she hardly recognized him. Wearing her best red dress Jane clung to Lilly both shared a look of despair covered with a smile of hope.

'You know Mr Humphreys is just down the hill,' he said, as he stood tall and tried to look brave, but his sweaty palms and shaking hands gave away his true feelings. They walked to the village together where the bus full of brothers, sons and fathers, destined to be soldiers, waited to leave.

'Please come back,' she whispered as he held her for a final goodbye. He kissed her and she held her breath trying to freeze that moment forever. Daniel turned and boarded the bus, women all around crying as the last seats were filled with loved ones. The men sat in silence, not blinking, just staring into the faces they were about to leave behind. Only sorrow and fear were their mutual companions now. As the bus pulled away, the grey skies let out a rumble, punctuating the misery of the moment.

*

The valley had changed through a season since Daniel was conscripted. Letters of love and hope filtered through and news that he had now finished his training and was to be sent to the trenches, in southern France. Correspondence from there was unreliable and horrific stories of the appalling conditions their loved ones lived in spread through gossip. It had been three months since Daniel's departure and Jane was thrilled to send him some wonderful news. She was pregnant. In his letters he appeared overwhelmed and it brought new hope for him. Only two months until Christmas, the dream of him being home began to fade from reality.

At Christmas the letters stopped. Jane was coming to the end of her second trimester and she needed help around the farm. Desperate to hear back from Daniel, she could not concentrate on anything, she paced up and down and played with her hair, today the post was late and she had a horrible feeling. She saw Mr Humphreys, struggling up the hill through the cold and the snow.

'Mr Humphreys what is it?' she hoped it was some village problem and not that dreaded yellow piece of paper.

Mr Humphreys' colour was not as blushed as normal, nor had she baked any scones today. As he said the words, 'Let's go inside my dear,' she feared the worst.

Inside by the warm fire, Mr Humphreys pulled out the yellow telegram. She stared at it unable to touch it, to make it real. She was grateful Mr Humphries was there, as he looked at her, she could see he cared and offered support. She sat in the chair - her chest tight, her breath rapid, she tried to not panic for the baby's sake. As she picked up the telegram her hands were trembling. Opening it, there was the news she expected- *'presumed dead'* were the only words she read. Nausea spread through her whole body, her breath became laboured, and everything went black.

'Jane? Jane? It's me Mr Humphreys. You've had a terrible shock my dear. Here I made you hot sweet tea, drink it please.' For a split second she forgot the telegram, then like a full speed steam train, it hit her again, taking her breath away for the second time.

Mr Humphreys held her hand and fed her tea. Jane felt like she was underwater, distorted noises and vision all around her. Inside she felt like her soul had been ripped out.

'How will I cope?' she muttered through agonizing tears.

'Right now, you must grieve. You will cope my dear. You have Lilly and that wee one.' His kind words were a comfort to her. He was the father she never had.

'Oh God, Lilly!' Jane stood up, but her legs gave way.

'Don't fret. Mrs Humphries has gone to fetch her.' He urged Jane to drink more, while he stroked the back of her hand, tutting, shaking his head every now and again and uttering the words *'tragic'* and *'loss'*.

Jane could not move. Mrs Humphreys had been looking after Lilly for a day now. She knew Lilly needed her mother, but she couldn't face the questions from her daughter. How was she to explain to Lilly that she no longer had a father? She closed her eyes again, to try and blank out the grief encompassing her. Jane jumped at a knock on the door.

'Go away.' She didn't care who it was, she didn't want to face the world.

'Jane, its Amanda. I'm not going anywhere until you've opened the door, besides its freezing out here.' Amanda was Daniel's sister and Jane knew she was a persistent woman. Amanda had lost her husband too only six months before with the war, and Jane felt that of all people she would understand her anguish after all she had now lost her brother.

Wrapped in a patchwork blanket, she shuffled her way over to the door. As she opened it Amanda pushed her away inside. Jane staggered back about to make some comment when Amanda grabbed her and held her tight. Jane felt her muscles relax throughout her body and allowed Amanda to hold her for as long as possible. The two of them spent hours in front of the fire reminiscing and cuddling, sharing their grief. Amanda declared she was here to stay. Jane needed help around the farm and instead of hiring someone, Amanda was determined to take on the role. Jane was grateful to not be alone anymore.

*

It had been over a year since Daniel had given her that final tender kiss. Jane's son was born in March and was a beautiful boy names Daniel Junior Collins, his eyes were brown like his father's and Lilly's. Now six months old Lilly enjoyed pushing him around the farm telling tales of her father, the hero. Amanda stayed and worked the farm while Jane cooked and cared for them all. She began to feel happy again. She had so many wonderful reasons to be fulfilled but the loss of her love, would never let go of that pain in her stomach, although she found it easier it was still there.

Jane and Amanda grew closer, becoming good friends. Apart from Mr and Mrs Humphreys Jane was happy to never see anyone from the village or even go there, not until the war was over. She wanted to remember her husband as the farmer he was not the soldier he died as.

Jane sat on the porch relaxing to another glorious summer sunset. Daniel Junior lay fast asleep in his crib, and Lilly and Amanda still down the fields. Her mind was playing tricks on her again. Often she would see a man walking in the fields or around the paddock. She knew it was nothing, but this evening this silhouette of a man was different. He climbed the hill with the sun behind him, this man walked with a limp and used a stick, and his posture seemed older. Jane got to her feet and shaded her eyes to try and see clearer who this stranger was. She got up unsure of what to do as a stranger headed towards her, she never had visitors.

'Hello. What do you want?' she yelled, unable to see his face from the glare behind him.

'To sit on the porch with you. To kiss you. To hold you and meet my son and cuddle my daughter.'

'Dan... Daniel!' Jane could make no volume, her heart raced and her legs began to run without hesitation. She flung her arms around his neck breathing in the smell of his skin as she held him so tight, she felt her soul rush back into her body as her life was complete again.

Jonathan Leong was born in the country of Malaysia, growing up amidst the embrace of books and stories from a young age. He began writing at the age of 10, and through a love of the arts, developed his writing abilities until his university days. A typical teenager, he enjoys reading, writing, gaming, and spending time with friends. He has interests not only in the writing arts, but also the performing arts, having joined school and college musicals in the years 2007 and 2009.

Jonathan Leong is currently a student, enrolled in the School of Law at the University of Bristol. Although he has attended multiple classes and clubs for creative writing, he has not previously been published. This short story, Desire, is his literary debut, his first work to enter publication.

Desire

Alzhamerim is a city of many things. It is a city of absolute power, with its looming castle surrounded by gleaming white marble walls rising high like a monolith from the center of the capital city, forever serving as both the symbolic guardian and dictator that stands over all of the empire. It is a city of both wealth and poverty, with its immaculately maintained high-rising spires that seek to touch the heavens inspiring the grandiose walls and gates that surrounds the city; even the city itself is arranged to reflect this difference, with rising tiers of land whose buildings turn from shacks and wooden houses to mansions and churches the closer they get to the castle, reflecting the position and worth of the people who lived in each layer of the city.

It is a city of stability and order, the glorious capital of a hegemony which conquered the entire world. It is a city of pride, and of prejudice, where the most noble of the nobles live, adored and exalted in their once chivalrous ways, while the rabble are scorned, cordoned and isolated off from the rich by the capital's inner walls, given almost no way to reach the city's inner sanctum. It is a city of crime, where murders and theft are the daily occurrences, and bribes are as common as authority abuse, hidden by the shadows of the night and of power, where no light can ever easily shine into.

Alzhamerim is all of those things, but above all, it is a city of brewing discontent, of unhappy people who are ready to boil over and take despicable matters into their own hands. It is a city on the verge of change.

Lyon Delacroix was ready for that change. It beckoned to him, almost tenderly, he felt, like how the flame beckons a moth to its roar. Although he was one out of many, he was special; he was the one noble that despised the hegemony of the Empire that provided for all nobles. In his eyes, the empire was prime to be torn down, rotting as it was in a never-changing stagnation that was as dead as the charred stumps of a forest ravaged by flame.

In his mind, change was a given, heralded by a faceless name that will go down in history as the father of revolution in the time of imperial dictatorship. However, he also knew that the name of Lyon Delacroix was not that name. Someone else would need to take the stage and spotlight, while he wrote the script that would be acted out, ever in the shadows.

Lyon was an outcast amongst the nobility, far removed from those who achieved their ranks from knighthood, and even more alien to those who were born of a lineage dating back to the First Empress. Though his rank of viscount, land, and fortunes were inherited, he would be the second generation of a family who had been sold their title, and the pure bred nobility disliked him for it. In fact, they resented him, alienating him from their culture and circles, ridiculing his family as insignificant, worth less than even the dirt they refuse to step on, or the forgotten shadows that trailed behind them, cast there by the uncaring light of providence known as The Empire.

None of that mattered. None of that mattered, for while they had squandered their lives in false abundance, indulging in luxuries stolen from the commonfolk, Lyon had been hard at work, gathering information on the state of the population, of the level of resentment the common-folk had towards the royalty, of the peasant's inspiration and heroes, people whom could rally them to their feet. He had been busy gathering like-minded people; land owners and entrepreneurs, lawyers and doctors, spies and assassins, actors in his little play to overturn the defunct system.

However, he lacked one important thing to complete the performance.

He lacked an army.

Seated behind the smooth contours of a well-shaped mahogany desk, Lyon Delacroix could not help but sigh at the senseless problem that he faced. He knew revolution could not be had without arms and bloodshed, and therein lay his biggest weakness; he knew no one who could gain that following of faithful believers, believers that would be prepared to set down their life for a greater good. He knew of swindlers and spies, assassins and murderers, soldiers and mercenaries that would die for money; but the fortune he was left with would never be big enough to field the arms he needed to defeat the Imperial Army. To try was to match a warhammer with a needle; not only would the weapon break, but the man wielding it would break as well.

It was the people themselves who had to rise up, for they were the only army large enough to face the Imperial Army that guarded the Empire. But for them to rise up, they needed an idol, a leader who would inspire them. Lyon knew of only three.

First, there was Firmin de Montanac, the hero of the middle-class. Successful entrepreneur, philantropist, the apple of the royal court's eye; he is the man who serves as the voice for those denied rank despite ability, believed to be fighting for equal rights for those who were capable. Believed to be, but in reality he was but a coward who pretends to stand up. He made a fine puppet of the government, and was paid handsomely to be so. Lyon knew he was as much a sham as he was useless, never possibly having the bravery to truly put himself at risk for a better future. He was just a figure of the status-quo.

Then, there was Count Remis Valerino, the star of the commonfolk. Born a peasant, the man had joined the Imperial Army as a mere conscript, working hard for thirty years. Not a decade ago the Imperial Army fought off raiding troll tribes in what is now known as The Southern Crisis, where he had gallantly saved the errant child of a duke of the royal courts. His heroic deed earnt him as position as commandant of a squadron of the city's guards, and the favour of the courts, while the Empress herself granted him the title of Count. His was a unique rags-to-riches story, a story and symbol of hope that even the commonplace may find greatness. Unfortunately, it was a story that promoted obedience to powers above your own; Valerino was too loyal to the courts for the favour they had bestowed upon him, and try as he might, Lyon was unable to see how the man may come to serve his purposes.

Finally, there was Dominic Seven, the enigma. He was a rebel, a vigilante that "served the people's interests", in his own words. The courts hated him; the peasants love him; the middle-class were indifferent. As much as Lyon would like to know more, there was no more to know. The bounty on his head was almost frighteningly high, the man having been blamed for an assassination attempt that had happened in the castle during the Empress' birthday celebration a fortnight ago. Being there as a member of nobility, Lyon could say that it was plausible that the man had hired help to do it, though it seemed unlikely a vigilante would go to such extremes. Either way, after the incident, Seven had all but disappeared into the night.

Lyon sighed with heavy fatigue, having gone through Seven's profile for the third time in that hour. A quick look around the room revealed very little; it was sparsely decorated, with nothing but pale peach wallpaper that covered the otherwise plaster walls. At the far end from the desk was the entrance, with two comfortable couches that lined up on either side for guests to peruse. Two chairs sat on the side opposite of Lyon, and atop his desk were stacks of parchment of various things: financial reports of the business he inherited, correspondences from his underworld contacts, schematics of certain key buildings in the city, and a score of other relatively minor issues that he could not be bothered with. Despite the importance of other matters, the man was wholly absorbed by the single piece of parchment in his hand; which was all the information to be bought off the black market regarding the enigmatic Seven.

As far as he could figure, this man was the key to Alzhamerim's uprising. However, there was inadequate information to do anything; there was no history to trace, no secrets to use as blackmail, and even contacting the man proved to be an impossible feat; no one in the criminal world of Alzhamerim knew where he was hiding, and most suspect he had long left the city fearing for his life. Although he was the best candidate, he was an impossible choice; one cannot make use of a tool that cannot be found.

Frustration clawed its way up his chest, pushing yet another sigh from the viscount's lips. The sky outside was pitch-black; he had been working well into the night. Although toppling an empire was a feat that requires years of patience and constant work, it felt to him as though he was running out of time, that his window of opportunity was fast closing, especially with the disappearance of Seven. If he did not act now, he would not get another chance; this baseless suspicion, though embarrassingly illogical and impatient, chewed away at him during the day and during the night, frustrating him more than any incompetence or issue that has plagued him since birth. Worst of all, it confused him; he was torn between seizing his opportunities, recklessly risking everything he owned, and patiently waiting, biding his time for a perfect opportunity that might never come. It wrought hesitation and inaction upon him, and every entrepreneur worth his salt knows that both are the roots of almost all utter failures.

His thinking was interrupted by a yawn; it was well past midnight, and the candlestick that served as the only source of light in the room was already nearly spent, so long had it been burning. It was a sign from the Maker that he should rest before the dawn-break prevented him from doing so.

Taking the candlestick from the desk, he retreated through the corridor that connected his three room apartment, gliding past the kitchen before opening the door that led to his bedchamber. What first occurred to him, that surprised him utterly, was the cold breath of wind that swept in from open double-door windows that swept out to his balcony, overlooking the Upper Circle marketplace; doors which he kept closed constantly, for fear of late night intruders.

That was his first hint that something was not right. The second thing that alerted him to another's presence was that there was a woman who was walking in from the door.

The candlelight played a soft glow that outlined feminine

BEST & BRIGHTEST 2012

contours on the silhouette, its rays not strong enough to penetrate fully the layers of dark and shadow that separated the two people in the room. She wore a catsuit of black cloth that seemed to absorb the light from around her, with skin-tight fitting that neither lies nor hides its owner's physical endowments. Her face shrouded in shadows, he did not recognise her until they came closer, her steps taken with forceful determination, his with fearful trepidation. His grip on the candlestick tightened.

Their steps stopped when they were close enough that the gentle glow of the candle caressed her face, bringing into light her mahogany brown hair, her snow white complexion, and her compelling green eyes that marked her as an acquaintance he was familiar with.

"Lady Gwendolyn?" His voice offered a weak welcome to the recently succeeded Baroness de Courtenay. To his mind, the question was that of confusion: what would a lady of the court be doing there? The answer was simple: a lady of the court would not be there.

She was a spy.

"What do you want?" His voice turned steely and hard, distrustful of his new intruder and her newfound identity.

She heard the distrust in his voice, and found it amusing; an amused smile stretched her lips, but she had neither the time nor the patience to deal with such things, as pressed for time as she was.

"Good evening, monsir Delacroix. I trust you have some moments to spare?"

She was confident. She was far more confident than befitted a woman, bordering on the precipice of pride. But in the dark world of a spy, it was necessary to know when to be as submissive as a shadow, or when to be as abrasive as a blazing light. When one comes to make a bargain, one must be as confident as an equal, and become the superior if possible. Calmly, composedly, she sat herself down on the edge of his satin bedsheets, crossing her legs with natural, cat-like grace.

"I have a little problem that I need your help with. I promise you'll be handsomely rewarded."

"Oh? Straight to business, milady? I thought the courts enjoyed to fill their greetings with comments of the passing weather and other such matters, before getting to the point."

She crossed her arms as well as her legs, keeping a sharp eye on the man's mannerisms and body language. He seemed to have relaxed, judging by the slump of exhausted shoulders and the free hand on his hip, but his eyes remained distrustful, suspicious. With certainty, his words were an indirect jab at her alternative identity. To humour him was best.

"Indeed, that would be one of the reasons the courts are such a dull place to spend one's time. Without question, my time is much better spent in the company of capable men, is it not, Monsir?"

A smile crept up his lips. She smiled as well, putting on the facade of the charming baroness she was known to be, knowing it would put him at ease.

"Likewise, milady. Your tongue is sweeter than honey, as it always is. But surely, a visit in the dead of night may be... misunderstood?"

His lips said misunderstood, but his eyes said provocative,

with how they hungrily roamed the contours of her feminine body. She leaned back, both hands pressed onto his satin bedspread, leaving nothing to obstruct his full view.

If one is to perform, one should give their all to their performance.

"Oh but monsir Delacroix, some things are better done in the night, I believe, where there are no prying eyes and… disturbances." She winked provocatively at him, intending to edge him on to the point of incoherent thinking. Men have always been known to do callous and silly things for women.

"Surely you have no problem listening to a woman's little private request?"

"I'd be delighted to." he said eagerly, walking past her to shut the double-door windows. He would have dropped the drapes as well in misled anticipation, if not for the fact that her next sentence completely stopped him in his tracks.

"I want Seven broken out of prison."

Silence was all that transpired between them, Lyon looking over his shoulder at the dark silhouette that was no longer illuminated by gentle light nor savage flame. Things did not make sense to him, and her words repeated themselves in his head without end.

"You want… Seven… out of prison." he repeated hesitantly, breaking the silence with unsure footing. Unsure of where the conversation was going.

"...How do you know about Seven?"

"Who doesn't know about Seven? The dashing thief that steals jewels as well as he steals hearts; I think he would make a rather interesting pet to have, don't you?"

She offered the statement airily, a passing comment of no real consequence; she pulled off the act of an uncaring noble far removed from the weight of reality, with no grasp on what was reasonable, or possible.

But something was off. Something felt wrong with the scene, for it made no logical sense to the viscount at all. He let down the drapes, turning around to face her, but she kept her back to him, almost as if oblivious to his presence. It irked him. Despite that, he had to stay calm, for in the dangerous game of cat-and-mouse he had just engaged, any wrong move that irked his guest could end his life.

"Oh dear. The last I heard, Seven had left the city, scott-free." He advanced carefully, trying to dig out as much information from the dangerous woman he had essentially locked himself in with.

"Your prince has long left, milady."

"Well perhaps your sources are outdated, monsir. Seven is in the city, and he is in the imperial dungeons, ripe for the picking. I can confirm that more than your sources can."

She brushed her hair back while turning just enough for him to see the edge of her face, beckoning him with a few pats on the soft silk next to her.

"Come monsir, put down the candlestick and have a seat. The texture of your sheets is too beautiful to waste."

From the corner of her eye, she observed him walking back to her, uncertainty written all over his face. He was well-confused and disoriented, which gave her the perfect chance to push her advantage in their tug of war. A small feeling of victory rose in her chest from this knowledge, akin to the enthralling excitement that all spies felt when they see their prey fall into the pretty webs. It was the same as the traps that spiders spun to snare flies; intricate, beautiful and inescapable.

"This is such a good chance for you, monsir Delacroix. A chance to put the infamous Seven into your debt. A chance to obtain anything you want. He can do that you know. He can get anything… from anyone."

"Well perhaps he is not as talented as you believe. After all, he is in the dungeons now, is he not?"

Agitation weaved through his words, a rising annoyance that she managed to catch despite the man's best attempts that keeping his voice calm and level. She chuckled to herself, almost knowingly, prompting a raised eyebrow from him.

"You sound like a jealous man, monsir Delacroix." She cooed as she removed herself from the bed, lithely gliding over to the man before placing her delicate fingers around his arms, her chest pressed into his back. She felt him shudder from the contact.

"That's encingly attractive."

Her breath tickled his neck as she whispered the words into his ear, standing on tiptoe to reach. His restlessness and uncomfortable squirming, no doubt meant to discourage her proximity, only served to edge her on, sliding her fingers lower, until they caressed his stomach in ticklish circles.

"I might be more… inclined to visit again, if you do me this little favour…"

One hand found his belt, tugging on it slightly as a private suggestion, but he immediately pulled away from her touch, putting a good half dozen steps between them with hurried panic. His eyes, reflected from the light of his candle, showed the shadow of fear that lurked beneath the temptation of lust that she had been manipulating since she set foot in the room. Though the fact he had pulled himself away was unexpected, the night was still young; she had many more chances to chain him to her.

"Do you find me unsatisfactory, Viscount?" she pretended to be hurt, looking away with downcast eyes, thoroughly enjoying the act that she was playing.

"Do you not want me, here?"

"Why do you want Seven?"

"Why are you evading my question? Viscount, I did not think you the type to be rude to a lady."

She naturally lifted her head to face him again, discreetly searching him with her eyes from toe to head to find a change in body language or facial expressions. She almost scowled to find him back on one foot, fear having taken over from the primal, cardinal sin. What had she done to create such fear within him? Perhaps she had been overzealous in her approach?

She took a step forward towards him, but as she did so, he took another step back. It seemed that he was keen to keep his distance, fearful perhaps of the almost mesmerizing touch that she had. She herself was unsure of what to do now; would it serve her better to increase her aggressive approach, or to give him some space to breathe?

Uncertainty plagued her as much as it did him, but she had no time to be uncertain. Hesitation taints the moment worse than a wrong move; in a stand-off where both are as confused, the first person to make a move wins. Thus with vigour she pushed forward, forcing him to take steps back until he was pushed up against his wall, cornered. With slyness that would best a fox, she slithered up next to him, hand splaying with gentle sensations across his chest while on tip-toe, her mouth high enough to nibble his ear if she wished.

However, before she could act, he had already reacted, quickly brushing her hand out of the way as he side-stepped away from her seductive advance. Without hesitation, he marched across the room, putting as much distance as he could between him and her, before placing the candle down on his bedside table. Its steady but flickering gaze threw light everywhere in a gentle caress, but blocked by the man's folded arms, it could do no more than cast a wavering shadow that hid his face as well as the darkness hides hers.

"Let's make this clear, Gwendolyn. You're asking me to commit treason by raiding the imperial dungeons, in order to save a man that you want to have in your bedchambers. Leaving aside the disgrace that is, this deal is unbeneficial to me. I have no use of a thief."

"Oh come now, Lyon. We both know that you're very interested in Seven." her silky voice cooed to him, a distraction that was followed by her jaunty strides as she came closer to him, once again. She was unnervingly touchy, and Lyon almost missed the hidden emphasis she had placed in the word "very". Suddenly, the natural sentence did not sound as natural as it should have.

"Interested in Seven? How so, my dear Gwendolyn?"

"Oh come now, Lyon. We know all about your search for Seven and his secrets. Your informants are ours too, after all. We know all about your need for a public hero, a man that people recognise and respect enough to follow and your fascination with him for that precise reason."

Her smirk was barely visible in the light, a victorious smile that was sketched onto the delicate full lips that incessantly enticed him so. She was like a tiger; without mercy she advanced forward in her psychological assault, getting ready to pounce on prey the moment weakness was shown. Lyon knew this. As helpless as a cornered rabbit, it was all he could do to keep his calm, to restrain the growing hunger he could feel from the very depths of his body.

Stay calm. Stay calm. Stay calm. Think.

"We can help you start your revolution, Lyon. And it will be a beautiful thing."

"We?"

He uttered the first thing that came to his mind, desperate to find an angle that would let him shift her focus. Logically, he could just walk out of the room; there was nothing that prevented him from doing so. However, her charms were too great, and it was next to impossible to fully remove himself from the situation that she was putting him into. To do so would take a strength of will so great that it would rival that strength of mythical dragons. More so than that, there was a dreadful feeling that, if he refused her there and then, it would be the end of him.

Questions bogged down his mind. Why now? Why him? Why Seven? There must surely be something going on, and something that will likely not end well for him. Those were the things he must find out, before the spy robbed him of his sanity, his free will, and his life.

Already he could feel his own will slip away, thoughts constrained by his desire for her. It was like a losing battle, before he was even able to begin fighting.

"Oh dear, I said 'we', didn't I? Well, I suppose it won't hurt for you to know."

She seemed to glide to the bed, her footsteps making no sound on the carpeted floor; she was a shadow that crept silently through the edges of light, never content with staying in one place for long.

"Seven and I are both part of a… network of spies. An organization, with the goal of usurping the throne of the empress. We want the same thing, Lyon. Help us, and we'll help you."

She crossed her arms, smiling smugly. It was obvious that she was in a position of superior negotiation power; she had all to offer him, and he, only this one service. It would be easy to do so; he possessed a copy of the original blueprints for the castle's interior, sold to him by the family that had first planned the monolith centuries before. Things such as that was easy to obtain when one party was facing financial disaster. All that would be left was for some hired hands to infiltrate the dungeons, grab the keys, let him out, and leave the way they came.

It was almost too simple to do.

"What exactly will I be getting, lady Gwendolyn?"

"Is a young maiden not enough for you?" she sighed, waltzing over to him with as much deliberate poise as she could and ran her fingers from his stomach to his chest. It was all he could do to close his eyes, chanting over and over again in his mind to remain calm. It was all he could do to keep himself from pushing her to the bed and ravaging her right then and there. Curse this woman, who tempted and tested a noble's dignity and honour!

"You are offered both a woman's innocence and your dream of revolution, and you want yet more? You are such a greedy man, Lyon."

"It is not greed, milady. Just making the terms of the contract clear."

"Contract? What a dull word! Is there no passionate word you could use for our little affair?"

She sighed, detaching herself from him to marvel at the workmanship put into the crafting of his four poster bed. Her hand trailed gently on the wooden post closest to her, seemingly engrossed in the smooth textures and the stylistic patterns carved into its body. So engrossed was she, that it seemed as if she had forgotten about Lyon entirely.

Of course that was part of the trick; shifting from being fawned over to being ignored was disorientating at best, upsetting in most cases. It would be easier to trip him up, confuse him until he unwittingly pledged his help to her cause. From then on, the noble's own code of honour would do the work, binding him to his own promises.

It was a game of cat-and-mouse. She was the cat.

"It's very simple. You do this, you will get the head of your peasant army, the man who you think can lead the people to stand up against the Empire. You get our help with information, secrets, and deception you need to pull off your designs. For a price, of course. If that is not enough, I am willing to share some of the Courtenay fortune with you... depending on how well you succeed."

"Do I not get the company of a beautiful maiden?"

"That depends on how impressed I am, monsir Delacroix. Do we have a deal?"

She winked suggestively as she put out her hand. Surely instead of a handshake, she expected him to kiss her hand; a romantic, cavalier gesture not uncommon to the ranks of nobility. He was sorely tempted to; with little cost to himself, and with so much to gain, it almost seemed too good to be true.

He extended his hand, about to take hers into his.

But something did not make sense. Something chewed at him, whispering into his ear that she had not told him the truth as it should be. She and Seven were both from an organization of espionage; that was believable, considering the ease that she had entered his domain, and the way she seemed to glide and remain soundless as she had walked about the room like a wandering spirit. But it made no sense to him why Seven would have let himself be caught, when even the underworld was unable to find him, or why this woman had now come to him for help.

It made no sense at all.

"No... No we don't. Because you don't need me for this."

His words started out quiet, but were quickly rising in volume, picking up the pace as things suddenly fell into place. The puzzle that formed the picture, the scene, had its last piece revealed to him, clearing out the fog of confusion that he had been subject to ever since she stepped into his room.

"You don't need me to rescue Seven. You are from a powerful, a knowledgeable organization; you should know everything about everyone, have people everywhere. You are the first to know if something is going to happen, and the first people to take advantage of it. You don't need a third party like me to get him out of prison."

Enlightenment dawned on his face, and his outstretched hand turned to point accusingly at the woman as he reached a crescendo.

"You need my help because you don't have your organization's backing. Seven isn't important enough to them to risk whatever it is you want them to do. That's why you need me. You're desperate."

She scowled. He had hit the jackpot.

The balance of power had now shifted to Lyon; he was now the cat instead of the mouse. As her scowl deepened while he smiled triumphantly, it was obvious she realized this too.

"You make too many assumptions, monsir. I assure you, my visit to you is out of favour, not need. You are not that special."

"Then you are free to leave. The door is that way."

He gestured to the balcony windows with overwhelming bravado, that smile still etched into his face. At first all she could do was to stare in disbelief at his newfound arrogance, slowly registering that he was accepting her challenge. Eventually though, she removed herself from the bed, walking with indignant steps towards the glass window that she had entered through in the first place.

Shoving aside the drapes and pushing the window open, she

made to leave with as much grace as she had entered. Lyon feared he may have made a wrong choice; it was wholly possible he had deduced the situation wrong, and if so, he was throwing away his chance of a lifetime.

It was frightening to think so.

The tense anxiety and anticipation he held his breath with lasted for what felt like an hour, or a day. Ideas and words raced through his mind, of what he could say to dissuade the lady from leaving, as she wavered at the impromptu exit to his room. Words of command, persuasion, ideas of temptation, negotiation, and of possible recourse should he mess up.

It was all wasted effort, for after the eternal moment, as she stepped a foot out of the room, the window was slammed shut with enough force to rock its foundations. She stood inside the room, irritated and angry visage hidden by the shadows she had retreated to when she tried to leave.

"Fine. Yes, I'm desperate. I'm desperate enough to come to you for help. I'm desperate enough to go to the only noble I know who is trustworthy and not blinded by the false worth of their heritage. I'm desperate enough to ask a real man for help."

Angry was her voice, filled with loathing for how she was reduced to begging. A strong woman, it was no wonder that she seemed hardly able to accept the thought. But accept it she did, with as much humility as she could muster. Her voice softened, and she came back into the weak light, meek and calmer than but a moment ago.

"Please, Lyon? I can't do this without you."

He smiled, but it was not a smile of mirth, or of friendliness. It was a smile of merciless victory, of self-assurance for absolute control that was partially hidden by a flick of the candle's shadows; he knew that she had no power left to demand, for it was all within his hands now. The only question was how much he could ask for.

"Milady, regardless of how you phrase it, you are asking for a tall order. To get into the castle is already hard enough, what with the increased security since Seven's attempt on the Empress' life. To get him out unseen-"

"That's a baseless rumour. Seven wasn't involved in that."

Her sudden outburst took him off-guard. A quick glance at her revealed nothing; she was calm, meek, and unflinching with her eyes closed; she was the perfect picture of meditation, as of that moment. He cast her a side-long glance, thinking about what she had just said.

"Then that makes him nothing more than a thief. A thief and a conman that spins false heroic tales of slaying dragons that have gone extinct, fighting undead armies that leave no trace, and dueling giants that are of myth. Why him?"

"Seven is not like that. You know it, and I know it. That's why you're looking for him, because you know people respect him. People will follow him. You need someone that can fill the role you cannot."

"I look for him," his voice flared momentarily, tone rising sharply in a sudden burst of almost uncontrolled anger at being disrespected by a woman. However, that was unacceptable; he cut himself short, taking a deep breath to calm his temper, before starting again with more poise.

"I look for him, because the people believe he does good. Robbing from the rich and giving to the poor? If anything, I would assume he tells these tales to woo the ladies, who are no doubt swooning over him in every brothel that he visits in this city-"

The flurry of action that interrupted him this time was faster than the eye could see. Before he knew it, he had been thrown against the wall, pushed up against it with the whole weight of a body, still slow to realize the sharp point of a knife kissing his Adam's apple.

Silence was all that transpired between them, with tension so thick that it hindered his breathing as much as fog. Nothing needed to be said; the feelings that came across in the impulsive action, the knifepoint, and her deep breaths was more than enough to replace words.

"You love him," he said, realization dawning on him.

"So that's why you're desperate. That's why you're looking for help from an outsider. You're afraid of him dying. You're afraid of him being executed, used as an example of those who oppose the Empire. That's why there are rumours of him attacking the Empress, and that's why he's not dead yet. It all makes sense now."

She replied with silence, her steady hands on his neck and knife no longer so steady. Seeing her calm demeanour falter, and knowing without doubt the reason for it; feelings of jealousy rose in his chest because of it. Jealous that it was a rogue and thief that commands people's love and respect, not him.

It wasn't fair.

It never was fair.

"Let go of me." His words were short, soft, and straight to the point.

Grudgingly, she did so.

Suddenly, darkness enveloped the two. The candle had worn out the last of its wax, sitting in a clear puddle at the bottom of its lamp, having no wick left to burn. In the dark, neither could see the other; and the lady failed to see the contorted faces of anger that swept through his face in intervals as he tried to keep himself calm.

"My conditions are as follows."

His solitary voice was the only thing in the room; nothing else seemed to exist, as dark as it was, and as silent as it was. With the drapes down, there was no moonlight to filter into the room, regardless of how little there was out in the dark, cloudy night to begin with.

It was just the two of them.

"Seven will be the new leader of a peasant army, one that he will be building from the population of Argenion."

In a dark room.

"You, on the other hand, will be my liaisons with your organization. That will go exactly as you suggested it, but I want you to carry out any deeds I need done to people."

The bed was but two feet behind them.

"The one addition I make, is that I want the fortunes of the Courtenay family to be mine. Legally."

She kept silent, considering her proposal. Perhaps it was a blessing that it was pitch-black, so that the man could not see the look of sudden shock and revolt that took her face.

"That would mean that I... would have to marry you."

"Smart girl."

"That is more than just scandalous, viscount. That is downright atrocious. Do you take joy in torturing women like this? I cannot accept."

"I will not change my conditions. Accept, or Seven dies."

His heartbeat rose with every word, the tension he was feeling only exaggerated by the rising feeling of excitement that invaded him with the knowledge of what he was doing. It mattered not that she kept silent, making even her breathing invisible to all senses; he knew the eventual answer she would be forced to give.

"I consent, viscount. Now, if I may take my leave..."

She turned to go, but Lyon would not let her. Before she could move properly, she felt herself being pushed backwards, tripping and stumbling from the shift of balance to fall onto the bed. Almost immediately after, the weight of a man mounted her.

"What are you doing!? Don't touch me!"

"Is it not normal for a husband to indulge in their wives?" he said viciously as he fought to pin both her hands under the weight of his body. He was not very successful.

"I would never sleep with a man like you! Get off me!"

The sound of struggling was suddenly replaced by the loud smack of flesh against flesh. Her struggling stopped, as did his, while she caressed the cheek that he had slapped.

"What was all that you were saying before then? Were you merely lying from the moment you stepped into my room, in order to get my cooperation, then planning to disappear with your prince into the sunset? I am an entrepreneur before a noble. I will not walk away empty-handed. Consent, or the last time you see your lover will be on the execution block."

He would not see it, distracted as he was by his own rising desires, but tears slid down from her eyes. She cried silently, trapped between losing her dignity or losing her love.

"You're a monster, Lyon. A heartless monster."

Her body slacked, ending all resistances to his assault.

Without a word, he leaned forward to take a breath of her scent, the fragrance of her hair and exposed neck, while she cried silently, hopelessly, beneath him.

"I won't be left empty-handed," he muttered absently, indulging himself in the object of his primal desires for the night. He did nothing wrong; she had come into his bedroom, tempting and tantalizing him before the tables were turned on her. She had brought this upon herself. Moreover, she was doing it to save her lover.

Seven. The name brought a tint of jealous hatred to him, and the surge of emotions brought out an act of passion that made her gasp, though not necessarily from excitement. Despite that, he felt himself only more aroused, intoxicated perhaps by the feeling of power and dominating others.

Trapped within the throes of his own guilty pleasures and his own intoxication, he could not help but think one thing:

It would be a beautiful night.

Copyright Information

You've read the rest, but whose is best?

We're asking YOU. Please rank our contributors' pieces of work, from #1 (top) to #10 (bottom). The author whose work gets rated most highly by the most people will claim the prize of BEST & BRIGHTEST 2012 PEOPLE'S CHOICE!

FINAL CANDIDATES (Students & Graduates)	RANK #1>#10
Aedan Andrejus Burt's WHISKY	
Charles Eades' JANUARY BRINGS THE SNOW	
Richard Willis' HEREDITARY INSTINCT	
Julia Lacey Brooke's THE HAUNTING OF DAISY THOMPSON	
Samuel Esau's BIRTHRIGHT	
Lydia Keys' BETRAYAL IN THE BLOOD	
Harry T. Greatorex's O'ER BOTH YOUR HOUSES	
Ben Wright's THE WOMAN OF THE TOWER	
Lilly Roberts' TOUCHED BY WAR	
Jonathan Leong's DESIRE	

Your votes are much appreciated, and can be sent to us either by posting this voting sheet to the address provided (see next page), or by going online and emailing your vote to bestandbrightestcompetition@gmail.com.

To:

Best & Brightest Competition Votes
New Dawn Publishers Ltd
292 Rochfords Gardens
Slough, Berkshire
SL2 5XW
United Kingdom

www.ingramcontent.com/pod-product-compliance
Lightning Source LLC
Chambersburg PA
CBHW050938120626
46552CB00001B/266